TWO LINES

Two Lines Press

TWO LINES   WORLD WRITING IN TRANSLATION
XXI, FALL 2014

Two Lines Press

Editor: CJ Evans
Senior Editor: Scott Esposito
Production Editor: Jessica Sevey
Associate Editors: Emmy Komada and Marthine Satris
Editorial Assistant: Ali Bossy
Founding Editor: Olivia Sears

Design by Ragina Johnson
Cover design by Quemadura

TWO LINES
Issue 21
© 2014 by Two Lines Press
582 Market Street, Suite 700, San Francisco, CA 94104
www.twolinespress.com

ISBN: 978-1-931883-37-5

Library of Congress Control Number: 2014934780

To subscribe to *Two Lines* visit www.twolinespress.com or mail a check to the address above. Subscriptions are $20 per year, individual issues are $12.

Two Lines is distributed by Publishers Group West.
To order for your bookstore call: 1-800-788-3123

This project is supported in part by an award from the National Endowment for the Arts.

ART WORKS.
arts.gov

Editor's Note

Twenty years ago, there were very few venues for translated literature in English, and those handful rarely paid much attention to the translator beyond, at best, a brief acknowledgment. In the first issue, we wrote about *Two Lines* as a forum for this overlooked work:

> We wanted to make a place for translation in which the act of translating was central. We wanted to share our work in a place where the contradictions and frustrations of translation were part of the ground rules.

Twenty years in, we are very gratified to have published more than 450 authors and more than 440 translators from 70 languages—but also to have helped spark what is still the beginning of a broader move toward publishing international literature and celebrating the art of translation. It is, first and foremost, the urgency and devotion of translators themselves that drive the burgeoning dialogue in the U.S. surrounding international literature in translation. And so with this, issue 21, we move to publishing *Two Lines* twice a year, to keep up with that vital and expanding conversation.

Despite all the new energy and effort devoted to the field, unfortunately, an absurd imbalance remains in publishing—the tsunami of American books that flood the markets around the world still dwarfs the trickle that translators and publishers manage to bring into English. And as the entire publishing industry continues to evolve, it is difficult to know what to expect when we look back again in 20 years.

This much, however, is certain: *Two Lines* will remain dedicated to finding dazzling new and underrepresented voices, brought into English by the best translators, and committed to celebrating the art of translation.

—OLIVIA SEARS, FOUNDING EDITOR

Contents

FICTION

Roger Lewinter	2	*Passion*
Rachel Careau	3	Passion
Alejandra Laurencich	38	*Los dinosaurios no han muerto*
Victoria Pehl Smith	39	The Dinosaurs Have Not Died
Antonio Tabucchi	92	*Controtempo*
Martha Cooley & Antonio Romani	93	Against Time
Hon Lai Chu	140	*Lin Mu yizi*
Andrea Lingenfelter	141	Forrest Woods, Chair

MEMOIR

Marcos Giralt Torrente	120	*Tiempo de vida*
Natasha Wimmer	121	Father and Son: A Lifetime

POETRY

Chika Sagawa	20	*Kaze*
Sawako Nakayasu	21	Wind
	22	*Yuki no mon*
	23	Gate of Snow
	24	*Butojo*
	25	Ballroom
	26	*Osoi atsumari*
	27	A Late Gathering
Shimon Adaf	28	*Aviva-lo*
Yael Segalovitz	29	Aviva-no
Søren Ulrik Thomsen	52	*"Den salte smag af dit kys kan jeg tydeligt huske…"*
Susanna Nied	53	"The salt taste of your kiss I remember clearly…"
	54	*"På de dårlige dage…"*
	55	"On the bad days…"
	56	*"For hver gang vi sås…"*
	57	"Every time we saw each other…"
	58	*"Mellem alle disse digte…"*
	59	"Among all these poems…"
	60	*"31 december…."*
	61	"December 31st…."
Pierre Chappuis	74	*Ces brassées d'étincelles, ces braises*
John Taylor	75	These Armfuls of Sparks, These Embers

	78	*Démarcation de l'incertain*
	79	Demarcation of the Uncertain
	80	*Sur le qui-vive*
	81	On the Alert
Rafael Courtoisie Beyhaut	82	*El café*
Anna Rosenwong	83	Coffee
	86	*Las naranjas*
	87	Oranges
	88	*La cuchara*
	89	The Spoon
Henning Ahrens	106	*Briefe an den Wirt*
Mark Herman and Ronnie Apter	107	Letters to the Host
Anne Parian	132	*Monospace*
Emma Ramadan	133	Monospace

ESSAYS

Rachel Careau	12	The Trivial and the Sublime: Roger Lewinter's "Passion"
Johannes Göransson	62	"A Wash of Mimicry": On the Deformation Zone of Translation
Contributors	160	
Credits	164	
Index by Language	166	

Roger Lewinter has been a highly original voice in European literature and scholarship for more than 40 years, as a writer, editor (of Diderot and Groddeck), and translator (of Groddeck, Rilke, Karl Kraus, and Robert Walser). His books include L'Apparat de l'âme *and* d'inflexion, pénétrant.

Passion

Un camélia auquel je m'identifiais—placé, dans le salon de mes parents, en face de mon bureau—, en novembre 1978, une semaine après la mort de ma mère, avait séché sur pied, perdant ses feuilles soudain—je l'avais offert, une dizaine d'années auparavant, pour l'anniversaire de mariage de mes parents, un 27 décembre—, cependant qu'un second camélia, acheté, pour la même circonstance, l'année suivante, et que ma mère, six mois plus tard, alors qu'il dépérissait—je disais qu'il faudrait le jeter bientôt—, sans avoir la main verte mais s'obstinant, avait su ramener à la vie, gagnait en force; dès lors, au scandale m'étant mépris, lanciné par l'impulsion d'acheter un camélia qui restaurât le premier, dans la mesure même où le second répondait—en décembre 1980, et tandis que ses boutons, jusque-là, tombaient, un coup de foudre m'exaltant, il avait donné deux fleurs longuement s'épanouissant; pour refleurir, régulièrement, quand je l'eus emporté chez moi, en novembre 1982, peu avant la mort de mon père—, me retenant: celui, toutefois, que je vis, le 1er février 1986, à huit heures du matin en allant aux Puces, dans la devanture de Fleuriot, me rivant sur place—il s'agissait d'un arbuste de plus d'un mètre de haut, non, simplement, d'une tige fleurie de la taille d'une azalée, comme les autres—, je résolus de laisser le sort trancher; car, cherchant quelque chose ...

Passion

A camellia with which I identified—placed, in my parents' living room, opposite my office—, in November 1978, one week after the death of my mother, had withered on the stalk, suddenly losing its leaves—I had given it to my parents, a dozen years earlier, for their anniversary, one December 27—, while a second camellia, which was bought for the same occasion the following year and which my mother, six months later, when it wilted—I said she ought to throw it out soon—, not having a green thumb but remaining obstinate, had been able to bring back to life, flourished; from then on, having misunderstood what is beyond understanding, gripped, to the same degree that the second responded, by the impulse to buy a camellia that would restore the first—in December 1980, and whereas until then its buds had fallen, a sudden passion elating me, it had produced two long-blooming flowers, to flower again regularly when I had taken it home with me, in November 1982, shortly before the death of my father—, restraining myself: the one, however, that I saw, on the first of February 1986 at eight o'clock in the morning on my way to the flea market, in front of Fleuriot, riveting me on the spot—it was a shrub more than three feet high, not simply a flowering stalk the size of an azalea, like the others—, I resolved to let fate decide;

because, looking for something that would motivate me to occupy the apartment next to mine, which had served for eight years as a storage room—the connecting wall had been broken through the previous May, without my having taken the next step—, I envisioned buying an antique Chinese rug whose dimensions corresponded to those of the corner room, which I thought I would fix up first—the owner of the rug wanted to get rid of it for health reasons, and when someone had spoken to me about it in January, on impulse I had said I would take it for a thousand francs—the price was around five thousand francs—, the negotiations being thus entered into, through an intermediary, without my having seen the rug—, the following Thursday a meeting having at last been set for Sunday morning, when, Saturday the fifteenth, in the afternoon, the owner let it be known that the rug had just found a buyer; making up my mind then to take the step.

When the camellia was delivered, on Monday at eleven o'clock, in the desire to enjoy its flowering, instead of putting it in the corner room, for which I had intended it—it was very cold and the apartment was unheated—, I put it in the kitchen, against the corner of the cupboard, halfway turned between the window and the counter on which was set, next to the sink, the other camellia, whose austerity it accentuated by its profusion, obviously giving umbrage—the sun came around to shine on them early in the afternoon—, because the next evening, after I had, as usual, smoked a last cigarette sitting crosslegged on the arm of the caved-in couch, opposite the little camellia, which I thus contemplated before going to bed, when I studied it I found that its two strongest leaves—those on which, a dozen years earlier, having read that one must devote one's thoughts to a plant for it to thrive, I had concentrated, so that they grew to the point of becoming, at twice the size of the others, disproportionate—, had died in the night: the dullness that had suddenly appeared on each side of the central vein—I knew it because I had observed it each time—, the depression hollowed out in the deep green thickness, spreading to the entire leaf, which, withering, in two or three weeks would fall; while the first reaction of the new camellia was to lose, almost immediately, most of the flower buds that studded it—but evidently artificially forced, it had had too many, and their fall could have been normal, since camellias react this way to a change of position while in bloom—; so that I was asking myself whether, once it became acclimated, it would still produce, despite everything, a flower—their color, deep crimson bordering on purple, seemed to me as exceptional as their form, opened out flat—without the crumpled petals at their heart like those of a peony—, like the roses of medieval illuminations—, when one of the surviving flower buds, among the smallest, on the overhang of the curved branch that formed the prow of the tree—situated at my eye level when, sitting at the low round table, I gazed at it as I ate—, seemed after a week's time to want to bloom, without managing to open, for as soon as the stamens sprang up from the half-open corolla, the calyx unfolding toward the bottom, the upper petals grew horizontally, like a visor, while the lower petals atrophied like a ruff—it was in fact two flowers joined together, the second of which took shape as the first opened—, continuing to hollow out at the bottom as they flared backward, torn apart by a proliferation of stamens; while scarcely ten days after its arrival—this also explained the dropping of the flower buds—, the leaf buds exploded, branches and leaves crossing impetuously, though the location near the window wasn't suitable—under the sun's rays the new leaves languished, only to recover in the evening, after a watering—; so that, no other place in the kitchen proving to be any better—the ideal position was facing east: in the corner room of the other apartment—, I finally put it in my office—there had never before been a plant there—, in the corner formed by a book cabinet that, in the afternoon, shielded it from the direct sun: next to the octagonal table where I write, to the left behind me, spreading out as if leaping, rising up slender, protective.

In March, on the first warm afternoon, the kitchen was invaded by moths—many came out from behind the cupboard, fluttering around between the branches of the camellia that was still there—, which—since they were what I feared most, because of the Kashmir shawls covering the walls of the bedroom and the office—I refused to perceive as such—not imagining that such a horde could hatch out in March, not giving any thought, moreover, to this invasion—, soon even giving up crushing them when, practically familiar, they threw themselves against me; a few days later, while moving the camellia, organizing the tangle of connecting wires of the stereo system under the counter—where lie spread, in the middle of a swath of empty matchboxes among the napkins and the silverware, tea, coffee, honey, cheese—, once again intrigued by the number of moths darting through the dust, too engorged or lazy to fly away; when, at the end of March, on returning from a reading in Paris of Kraus's texts, after lunch, during my nap on the caved-in couch, at the head of which, the previous July, before leaving for a Groddeck colloquium in Frankfurt and because it was extremely hot, in place of the two heavy wood crates containing some old 78s on whose account suddenly—they had been there for two years—I dreaded the sun's heat, I had set a big package of books, by Groddeck and about Groddeck, among them about twenty copies of *L'Apparat de l'âme*—it seemed to me more prudent to put the records in the books' place, in the shadow of the hallway—, noticing a maggot crawling on the metal foot of the low round table, I abruptly moved the big corrugated cardboard package: troops of larvae and moths, on the square of rug eaten down to the thread, were crawling at my bedside, not even scared off now by the light; and, the scales falling from my eyes, I realized that the kitchen was infested, the colony having swarmed over the half of the rug between the table and the window—the cracks between the tiles, under the rug, were infiltrated with cocoons, intact or frayed, maggots and eggs in clusters scattered everywhere—;

while in the entry, where I now examined the things hung in a heap on the coat hooks, with the exception of what I wore every day, everything was riddled—the previous summer, before throwing myself into the third Kraus, *Nachts,* I had told myself repeatedly that I had to straighten things up, but I had always postponed it, even though it weighed on me like guilt—; thus taking a month to fill garbage bags with soiled, disintegrating clothes—the Kashmir shawls, however, sprayed regularly each spring—the woolens rolled up underneath in a heap acting as initial bait—were practically unharmed—; relentlessly spraying walls, floors, baseboards, in the kitchen, the bedroom, the office, the hall; to discover, after a month, that the moths had taken refuge in the cupboards of the other apartment, where I had stored the few articles of clothing that had been spared; making up my mind then to throw out every superfluous thing made of animal fiber.

The camellia in my office, however, was thriving, and, the new branches luxuriant, it was soon encircled with an armor of foliage that, under the low-angled rays of the sun in late afternoon, lit up, wrapping like a subtle body the opaque mass of old foliage with a trembling into which, often, in the evenings, with exultation, I would plunge my face; nevertheless struck by the torment that appeared to flog its luxuriance—some of the leaves, among the oldest, were clipped, half-cut-away, but among the new ones, too, were many that, lifted up in the middle along the length of the central vein by a shriveling, were in contortions; and, branches bursting forth in all directions, in their intertwinings the leaves, when they didn't wind tightly around an obstacle, collided head-on and remained bound together in their opposite motion—, new leaf buds, not only on the trunk but also along the length of the branches, ceaselessly springing up and bursting open, like suckers on a rosebush; while already now—it was June—, the buds of flowers destined to grow plump in October revealed themselves everywhere, nevertheless very quickly starting to swell as if, in the urgency of fecundity catching up with the leaves, they would open at any moment; while with the idea—which had been on my mind since the beginning of the year—of finally translating the *Sonnets to Orpheus*, by Rilke—to which I had, in fact, committed myself by translating, two years earlier, the *Duino Elegies*, that the *Sonnets* might fulfill what the *Elegies* gave rise to: angel here below questioning, man beyond answering—, I read—with a determination incomprehensible even to me—*The Celestial Hierarchy*, by Dionysius the Areopagite, found at the beginning of July at the flea market, which, suggesting to me, to translate the word *Stille*—from which the *Sonnets* proceed—, rather than silence, impassivity, which, at the heart of suffering—its passion—, there seeing the beauty—objective, foreign—, knows its glory, the suprahuman rapture that it speaks through its surmounting, gave me the second word I had lacked until then—which I was, at the time, convinced was a given in French—and which, placed like a bolt in the first line of the first sonnet, thus laid it out—"Un arbre là monta. Ô pur surmontement"—, opening the entire cycle of the song of Orpheus, into which—"arbre haut dans l'oreille"—, after a few starts, on the twenty-fourth of August I threw myself as if it were now a matter of life and death; only occasionally worried about the camellia, beside me, which this struggle must have been irradiating even as it invigorated me; thus hardly surprised—noticing in it the sympathy I had sensed—that it began, in the course of the month of September, to lose some leaves—the most vigorous, which, majestic opened out, crowned its leader—, not worrying at first—their fall counterbalanced the luxuriance of the new leaves—, also seeing in it the repercussions of the uncontrollable development of the flower buds, which bent its branches and which, suffusing it with crimson, already burst open at the tips, which disconcerted me, although I recognized in it the sign of the frenzy rushing its cycles as if—and for a tree, which is truly its embodiment, this was a paradox—, for it, time didn't exist; while, as with the other camellia, I was letting the fallen leaves litter the soil—although under normal conditions they didn't decompose but, impervious to rot, withered—, when, moving them aside one afternoon to see whether I should water—it had been extremely muggy and hot for three weeks—, I found that the leaves that touched the soil were reduced to a network of veins; surprised—despite the varieties, there couldn't be such a difference between camellias—, so that—leaves more recently dropped on top of the others being likewise stripped of their tissue—, a few days later, to be clear in my own mind about it, I removed the mat: maggots, yellowish white, about a quarter inch long, crawling on the surface, immediately went back belowground; and removing the soil then with the tip of a leaf, I discovered yet another type of maggot, perhaps a half inch long, threadlike, translucent, like a fine rice noodle; and so, the insecticide sticks recommended by the florist seeming to me insufficient to check the likely proliferation of parasites—the leaves, invariably the strongest, of other branches were now decimated—, on September 23, reluctantly—dreading the effect on the swollen flower buds—, I applied a liquid pesticide—I had to water the plant with it, at the rate of one tablespoon diluted in a liter of water, three times at ten-day intervals—; the mixture absorbed, the soil—a sudden myriad of threadlike maggots, translucent, which lifted up twisting in every direction, contorting themselves in broken convulsions before slackening, struck down—heaved; and now, from everywhere, the yellowish-white maggots surged up, wandering across the surface, not dying instantly like the others; and two millipedes, driven from a clump of short branches at the base, streamed out, attempting to climb onto the trunk—so this was what I had found, ten days earlier, near the window, three feet from the pot, and had taken for a dead caterpillar—; faced with this devourment endlessly pouring forth—an hour, meanwhile, had gone by—, beginning to doubt that the treatment could be more than palliative—in the evening, by artificial light, the soil still shuddered—, and the second application, then the third, provoking the same cataclysm, I realized beyond any doubt that there was no other remedy than to transplant the tree—though this be fire and sword—, since the old leaves, pocked, fell in such numbers that wide gaps formed in the previously impenetrable thicket, while the flower buds, whose swelling had stopped with the first treatment, began to wither and soon fall as well; despite everything, still hesitating—I applied the pesticide six times—, when, in the middle of December—the *Sonnets* had been finished since October 5—, upon my return from a brief stay in Paris, discovering, in the evening, at the foot of the tree, the same teeming, I made up my mind and took the camellia, on December 18, to a horticulturist to whom I had presented the case, by telephone, at the beginning of November—in a *Tribune de Genève* from the summer, I had read an article on the alternative approaches he used to combat parasites, and unlike other nurserymen and florists, he had listened to me—, his diagnosis now confirming my own: it would be necessary, though it would have been better to wait till spring, to cleanse the roots and change the soil— that the rotting of the maggots was moreover poisoning—, and, he said, to cut back the tree because of the destruction of its roots; without my expecting that the camellia, when, on December 22, I came back to retrieve it, would be, broken lyre, the stump of its former self; while I had to wait a month, the tree living off its reserves, to know whether it would recover; two days after my return from a reading in Paris from *L'Attrait des choses*, on January 26 or 27, I don't know anymore, coming, in the morning, into the corner room—where I had placed it—to mist it, in front of its crushed leaves—at the beginning of January, one leaf bud having burst forth like a sucker at the base of the trunk, I had begun to hope—, I knew that in the night the tree had died, and that what would follow would be no more than the process of withering; coming into the kitchen, studying with increased attention the little camellia, the leaves of which, when I had taken the other one to the horticulturist, as if they had been tensed—the two trees, one in the kitchen, the other in the office, separated by the partition but at the same height, were back to back—, had seemed to me to spread out into their space; anxious that something might happen to it as well—for although it had two flowers, unlike the previous year's single flower bud, which had blossomed out fully on Christmas Day, they were only half-open—; suddenly concerned that instead of the five leaf buds corresponding to its five living branches, it had only three; thinking of giving it some fertilizer—only the previous year, and for the first time, because it was exhausting itself, I had added some peat moss and compost, to which it had responded with seventeen leaves, which had eased its destitution—; my worry increasing when, a few days later, I discovered that a small leaf on the long, leafy branch that, starting just above the soil, descended, greedily reaching for light through an ample bend, below the pot, had withered without my having noticed; deciding on the addition of the fertilizer when, the following week, from their dullness, I saw that one, two, three vigorous leaves were going to fall; stopping the treatment—the effect wouldn't become apparent for three weeks—on February 28 for the spring; that day spreading a tablespoon of salts—on this occasion, also breaking off the dead woody branches that, superstitiously, I had left, like a shield—; waiting: on March 20, from the dull gray of the exhausted leaves—for two weeks, they'd been stiff—realizing that it was too late; so that after three weeks' time, I put back in the kitchen of the other apartment, beside the dismantled shrub, the trunk burned to its pith.

The Trivial and the Sublime: Roger Lewinter's "Passion"

GENEVA, June 7, 2012. He lives on the fifth floor of an unremarkable walk-up opposite the Parc des Cropettes, in the Grottes Saint-Gervais neighborhood at the center of Geneva, just behind the Gare Cornavin. The stair to his apartment is almost circular, making the climb vertiginous, and I have to pause to catch my breath before ringing the bell at his door. Entering his apartment, you are immediately struck by the number of things scattered, set, draped, hung, piled, heaped, everywhere: books, record albums, paintings, porcelain figurines, Oriental rugs, tankas, etchings, drawings, photographs, everything found over a period of thirty or forty years at the *Puces*, the flea market. Papers lie everywhere in deep stacks. His collection of books is immense. But above all, the Kashmir shawls, which Lewinter prefers to call Kashmirs, the largest perhaps three or four feet by ten, the smallest four feet square: they cover the walls of the bedroom and the office, hang in the corner room and hallways, simultaneously radiating and receding, the botanical and paisley patterns of their borders, in crimson, vermilion, pale purple, sea green, turquoise blue, infinitely interlacing, at their center often a black square, octopus-like, its tentacles extending outward. Lewinter calls these Kashmirs "lieux de méditation"—places of meditation.

The apartment—it is in fact two apartments joined together decades ago—is cavernous, perhaps six or eight large rooms off long connecting hallways lined with tall bookcases. Everything he writes about in *Histoire d'amour dans la solitude* (Story of Love in Solitude) and *L'Attrait des choses* (The Attraction of Things) is there: the caved-in couch and the low round table in the kitchen, the octagonal writing table and the book cabinet, the clothes hung in a heap on the coat hooks by the door, the tangle of wires beneath the kitchen counter, the passage broken through the wall to the other apartment, all the Kashmirs he has described. Each object is carefully chosen, each object significant.

He is a small, slight, rather intense-looking man. When we meet in the lobby of my hotel just before noon, he wears jeans and a brown cashmere pullover and brown leather oxfords. Later, at his apartment, he sits semireclined on the caved-in couch in the kitchen, wearing brown leather loafers with white stitching, his feet curled up, as we have tea, which he drinks from a delicate porcelain cup without a handle, like a miniature Japanese rice bowl.

Roger Lewinter was born in Montauban, France, in 1941, to Austrian Jewish parents. The family entered Switzerland during the war, and Lewinter has lived much of his life in Geneva. Although his writing is often autobiographical and at times intensely personal, he is, para-doxically, a very private man, reluctant to talk about himself, his history. It is the work, the writing, that is important, and he has produced a great deal of it, as a writer, editor, and translator. He is the author of some dozen books, among them *Groddeck et le Royaume millénaire de Jérôme Bosch* (1974), *L'Apparat de l'âme* (1980; new edition, 1999), *L'Attrait des choses* (1985), and *d'inflexion, pénétrant* (2009). He is the editor of a fifteen-volume *Œuvres complètes* of Diderot (1969–73) and has produced, as editor and translator, a three-volume edition of the 115 *Conférences psychanalytiques* (1978–81) of Georg Groddeck, the German physician often called the founder of psychosomatic medicine, whom Freud credited as the source for his concept of the id (Groddeck's "It"). Indeed, the work of Groddeck has been central to Lewinter's creative output; besides the *Conférences*, Lewinter has translated six other works by Groddeck and is the author of an important study of Groddeck in German, *Georg Groddeck, Studien zu Leben und Werk* (1990). As a translator, Lewinter has ranged widely, translating works of psychoanalysis, art history, literature, and poetry by such authors as Ludwig Binswanger, Karl Kraus, Elias Canetti, Rainer Maria Rilke, Robert Walser, and Ramón Gómez de la Serna. He is the subject of a series of interviews conducted by Alain Berset, published under the title *en cours de phrase* (2002). In recent years, Lewinter has focused his attention on the study of prosody, and in 2009 he published an edition of Pierre Corneille's *Pompée*, the first to propose a prosody of this work.

I first heard of Lewinter in graduate school in 1989, when I was handed a copy of his recently published *Histoire d'amour dans la solitude*. That year, I completed a translation of the first, and shortest, story in the book, "Story of Love in Solitude." I wrote to Lewinter and sent him a copy, and he responded with a long handwritten letter, in English, addressing many particulars of word choice in the translation.

Around the same time, the journal *Avec* was assembling an issue devoted to contemporary writing in French, and they published "Story of Love in Solitude" in 1990. Having skipped over "Passion," I had already begun a translation of the third and final story in *Histoire d'amour dans la solitude*, "Sans nom" ("Nameless"), by far the most difficult of the three stories, since it comprises a single, long sentence (running to six manuscript pages), technically without beginning or end, progressing nonlinearly, through sophisticated syntactic play— Lewinter's "phrase sans point," a sentence without a period. I received another letter from Lewinter in June 1993, in which he again offered his assistance, since I had written to him, as far back as 1990, that

I was working on a translation of "Sans nom." The difficulties of translating that story, however, had seemed insurmountable at the time, and I think I had already set the translation aside by the time I received his letter.

I'm not sure what caused me to pick it up again fifteen years later, in 2008. I had worked as a freelance copy editor since 1994, and in part, it was that my work as a copy editor had begun to feel routine and I needed a new challenge; in part, it was also that I was no longer doing any writing of my own and wanted a means of reengaging with the process of writing. In the intervening years, I think several things had better equipped me to continue with the translation. Now forty-four years old, I had gained the patience and skills to work through challenges both emotional and professional. In particular, I had become accustomed to working through syntactic challenges, since much of my work involved untangling other people's sentences. Of particular help in approaching Lewinter's work, I think, was my personal reading, focused on eighteenth-century English literature—correspondence, journals, novels—which regularly exposed me to much more complex and varied syntactic structures than I encountered in my day-to-day work as a copy editor.

By April 2009, I had finished a draft of "Nameless" and wrote to Lewinter offering to send him the translation. A renewed correspondence between us ensued, Lewinter now always writing to me in French, and late in 2009 I sent him a draft of the story that appears here, "Passion." Lewinter's next letter voiced his concerns, not about the translation, but about the nature of *Histoire d'amour dans la solitude*, and of his book *L'Attrait des choses* as well, and how these texts could be understood in the absence of their original framework—literary, musical/lyrical, and, I would discover, spiritual—without which "the quasi-maniacal precision can only appear disproportionate in comparison with the triviality of the facts reported: moths, white and yellow maggots...." In my response, I wrote that the problems he raised are problems of translation generally, since a translation is always read outside the context of its creation; that the references—to Groddeck, Kraus, Rilke—are present in the text and therefore available to the attentive reader, so that the framework is not lost; and that a reader's experience of a text is always a process of discovery, to whatever extent the reader is willing to pursue that process.

Experiencing Lewinter's texts has certainly been a process of discovery for me. Beginning in 2008, I read a good deal of Groddeck, as well as secondary works about him, reread Rilke's *Sonnets to Orpheus* and *Duino Elegies*, attempted some Karl Kraus.

I did not hear from Lewinter for eight months. I wrote him another letter, to tell him that the translation of *Histoire d'amour dans la solitude* was coming along, to ask him about a perceived wordplay in the text of "Passion," and to let him know that I was interested in attempting a translation of *L'Attrait des choses* as well. This time, he responded quickly: "I was feeling annoyed with myself for having tried too hard to discourage you.... As for *L'Attrait des choses*: if you have the desire and strength to throw yourself into it, you must find a way to come to Geneva."

This invitation was what brought me to Geneva in June 2012. Lewinter wanted me to see the "things" in question in *L'Attrait des choses*; as it turned out, however, we spent the majority of my time there going over the translation of *Histoire d'amour dans la solitude* word by word in a series of sessions in his kitchen. I would arrive between two and three in the afternoon and leave around seven. We would work, we would break for tea, we would resume working. The procedure was this: sitting on a chair at the low round table, holding the text in my lap, I would read aloud my English translation while he, semireclined on the caved-in couch, followed along in the French, stopping me whenever something didn't seem right to him.

It was slow going. In our first session, we finished reviewing fewer than two double-spaced pages of manuscript in four and a half hours of work. Lewinter was very attentive to word choice, preferring, I think, Latinate to Anglo-Saxon words, so that to translate "laisser le sort trancher," for example, he preferred "to let fate decide" rather than "to let fate settle it." But he cared especially about the order of the phrases, insofar as it reflected the order of the intended perceptions and emotions they described.

The translation of "Passion" presented a number of difficulties, beyond Lewinter's complex syntax. In some places, a word-for-word translation wasn't adequate to capture Lewinter's sense in English; in others, I had overthought the translation, when a literal translation was called for but I had lacked the knowledge necessary to recognize it.

The first of the phrases that eluded me was "au scandale m'étant mépris." *Scandale* means scandal, scene, or fuss; *se méprendre* means to make a mistake, to be mistaken. So it could have meant something like "having been mistaken in making a fuss." I struggled to make sense of the phrase in context and sought help from native French speakers, who found the phrase no less puzzling than I did. In Geneva, Lewinter and I spent considerable time discussing the idea he was working with. It concerned the spiritual, a crisis of faith, he told me: that which the mind cannot comprehend had been miscomprehended, the enigma misinterpreted. He directed me to the work of Martin Buber and to the mystical writings of Saint Teresa of Ávila and Saint John of the Cross. Working on my own, I had entirely missed this spiritual meaning. I found reading the poems of Saint John of the Cross helpful, and ultimately I arrived at "having misunderstood what is beyond understanding."

Another instance of my missing the mark concerned the term *corps subtil*. Lewinter's text described luxuriant new foliage "enrobant tel un corps subtil" the older foliage of a camellia—wrapping it like a subtle body. But I had no idea what a subtle body was. I reached for an answer, and after discovering that *corps* can also mean a bodice or corselet and that *subtil* can mean delicate or fine, I arrived at "wrapping like a finely textured garment." Lewinter corrected me: *corps subtil* is a mystical term; I might find it in a yoga dictionary. He suggested I look at the work of Sri Ramakrishna. I discovered a copy of *The Condensed Gospel of Sri Ramakrishna* and found the term there: "subtle body," *sukshma sarira*, a concept in yogic philosophy. In this case, my own ignorance had caused me to go far afield in venturing a translation, when the literal translation would have been correct.

There was also an instance of wordplay. It concerned the relationship of two camellias, the more luxuriant of the two "portant ombrage manifestement," which I translated as "obviously giving umbrage." *Ombrage*, like its English cognate *umbrage*, can mean both shade and offense, and *porter ombrage* means to cause offense, to offend, but it could also conceivably mean to shade. What caused the slightest doubt to enter my mind was the phrase that followed, set off with dashes as though it were an explanatory element: "the sun came around to shine on them early in the afternoon." I knew that Lewinter had translated several works by Karl Kraus, the Austrian satirist, essayist, and aphorist who, among other things, was fond of puns. In a letter, I asked Lewinter to confirm my translation "obviously giving umbrage." He responded, "You are right: the French has the same double meaning as the English *umbrage*, and for me, it's a question of resentment/offense, injury, and not of shade." Translating *ombrage* as "umbrage," rather than "offense," preserved this double sense in the translation.

Perhaps the most difficult passage in "Passion" concerns Lewinter's own translation of Rilke's *Sonnets to Orpheus*. The text becomes quite dense and fragmented at this point, punctuated with multiple dashes setting off amplifying elements. The phrase "inhumain ravissant qu'elle dit par surmontement" posed multiple difficulties. Confronted with "inhumain ravissant," I wasn't sure how to orient myself; which was the noun, and which the adjective? The word *inhumain* suggested its English cognate *inhuman*, which is indeed its meaning as an adjective; as a noun, in archaic and literary use, it means "cruel being." *Ravissant* is an adjective meaning beautiful, ravishing, but it could also be the present participle and gerund (the present participle used as a noun) formed from the verb *ravir*, which, in a theological sense, means to be transported outside oneself by contemplation. *Surmontement* means the act of overcoming. I arrived at this conjecture: "that cruel being of ravishing beauty that it expresses through transcendence." In Geneva, Lewinter oriented me correctly: *inhumain* was the adjective, *ravissant* the noun—I had had their functions reversed. By *inhumain*, he had meant divine, beyond the human; by *ravissant*, rapture in the theological sense. For *surmontement*, he found the English word *transcendence* "false," preferring the word *surmounting*. In time, I arrived at "the suprahuman rapture that it speaks through its surmounting"—a "literal" translation of the phrase, but one informed by its sources in mystical thought and respectful of the preferences Lewinter had expressed.

The days spent in Geneva proved essential to understanding the nature of the text and thus to bringing the translation as close as possible, not just to the words of the original, but to the thoughts behind them. Lewinter had drawn my attention, most importantly, to the story's spiritual framework, which I had had difficulty both in apprehending and in finding the proper vocabulary to convey, and to the multifold spiritual connotations of its title, "Passion," so central to his intention in the text: joy, suffering, death.

Lewinter continues to visit the flea market regularly. There, as he has said in *en cours de phrase*, "le trivial et le sublime sont liés"—the trivial and the sublime are tied. "Pour moi, les choses spirituelle-ment importantes se sont manifestées aux Puces"—things that are spiritually important have revealed themselves at the flea market. Similarly, it is through the seemingly trivial—"moths, white and yellow maggots"—that the text of "Passion" speaks of the spiritual: "deux manières de voir une seule et même chose, de vivre une seule et même expérience"—two ways of seeing the same thing, of living the same experience.

Chika Sagawa, the pen name of Aiko Kawasaki, was born in 1911 in Hokkaido, Japan. One of Japan's first female Modernist poets, Sagawa's poems were posthumously collected by Ito Sei and published under the title Sagawa Chika Shishū *(Collected Poems of Sagawa Chika) in 1936.*

風

単調な言葉はこはれた蓄音機のやうに。
草らは真青な口をあけて笑ひこける。
その時静かに裳がゆれる。
道は白く乾き
彼らは疲れた足をひきずる。
枸杞色の髪の毛が流れる方へ。

Wind

Monotonous words, like a broken gramophone—
Grass laughs hysterically, with its bright green open mouth.
And then the skirts sway quietly.
The road dries into white
And the men drag their tired feet
To where the hair flows, red like wolfberries.

雪の門

その家のまはりには人の古びた思惟がつみあげられてゐる。
——もはや墓石のやうにあをざめて。
夏は涼しく、冬には温い。
私は一時、花が咲いたと思つた。
それは年とつた雪の一群であつた。

Gate of Snow

People's outdated beliefs are piled up around that house.
——Rather pale, like gravestones.
Cool in summer, warm in winter.
For a moment I thought flowers had bloomed.
It was a flock of aging snow.

舞踏場

私の耳のすべてで
私はきく
彼らが行つたり来たりしてゐる
胞子のやうに霧が空から降つてゐる
床の上のさわがしいステツプ
私は見た
花園が変つてゆくのを

Ballroom

With all of my ears
I listen
As they go back and forth
Their noisy dance steps on the floor
Like mist falling from the sky like spores
I saw it
The transformation of the flower garden

遅いあつまり

口笛を吹くとまた空のかなたからやつて来る。限りない色彩におぼれることの無 いやうに。エメラルドやルビイやダイヤモンドの花びらが新しい輝きに充ちて野 山をめぐる。うなだれる草の細い襞が微風を送る。テラスは海に向つて開かれ、数へ切れぬ程の湿つた会話がこぼれる。今はなく、時には鮮やかに。

A Late Gathering

I whistle and they come back from deep in the sky. As if they never drown in those endless colors. Emerald, ruby, and diamond flower petals roam the fields and mountains drenched in a new brilliance. Thin drooping folds of grass send out the slightest breeze. The terrace opens out to the sea, and countless damp conversations spill out. No longer, but at times vividly.

Shimon Adaf, a son of Moroccan immigrants, was born and raised in the Israeli Gaza border city of Sderot. The hyperinnovative secular Hebrew of his poems is saturated with biblical and Talmudic intertextualities. The collection Aviva-no mourns the untimely death of Adaf's sister.

אביבה לא

א.

אֲנִי בְּמַצָּב אֵיךְ לְהַגְדִּירוֹ וְאֶקְרָאֵהוּ אֲבִיבָה-לֹא אֶקְרָאֵהוּ אֵינָחוֹת
וַאֲדַבְּרָה בּוֹ יְשִׁירוֹת לֹא עַל דֶּרֶךְ הַשִּׁירָה אֶלָּא לְפִי כְּאֵב
וְזֹאת הִיא תוֹרָתוֹ אֵין לוֹ תוֹרָה–מַלְאָכִים מְחַנְּקִים נְשִׁימָה וְחַיּוֹת
בּוֹעֲרוֹת עֵינַיִם, בָּאִינְטֶרְנֶט מִמַּעַל וּבַסְּפָרִים הַנִּקְבָּרִים, אֵין
לוֹ תוֹרָה, רַק הָרֶגַע בְּעַצְמוֹת הֶחָלָל הוּא נוֹקֵב כְּסְכָּה בִּזְכוּכִית
וְהַלֵּב הֶחָדֵל וְקַרְנֵי הֶבֶל
מִשּׁוּם שָׁלוֹשׁ מֵאוֹת שִׁשִּׁים וַחֲמִשָּׁה מָנִים שֶׁל עָשָׁן שֶׁבּוֹ
כְּנֶגֶד שָׁלוֹשׁ מֵאוֹת שִׁשִּׁים וַחֲמִשָּׁה מִנְיַן יָמוֹת.

Aviva-no

1.

I'm in a state of how does it go and I shall call it Aviva-no I shall call it sisterless
and I shall speak of it with straightforwardness not by way of verse but by pain
and thus is its Law it has no Law—stifling-breath angels and blazing-eyed
beasts, in the internet above and in the buried books below, it has no
Law, it is only the moment piercing the power of space like a pin into glass
and the heart is arrested and named mere breath
for the three hundred and sixty five minas of smoke within it
against the count of three hundred and sixty five days of.

ד.

נִזְקַקְתִּי גַם לַגּוּף
שֶׁיְּשָׁבֵר
וְלֹא
נִשְׁבַּר
בָּאוּ סִיעוֹת צִפּוֹרִים
בַּבָּשָׂר
אַנְקוֹרִים חֲשׁוּיִּים בְּדָמִים דְּרוֹרִים
שְׂרָף נָטַף מֵעֲצֵי קֶטֶף
קְפוּאִים כְּמוֹ זְכוּכִית, זוֹרְחִים
כְּרָדִיד נַיְלוֹן
תַּחַת יָרֵחַ מֻשְׁלָךְ בָּאַשְׁפָּה
חָדַלְתִּי מֵרְאוֹת
אֵיךְ אֶחְיֶה
בַּחַיִּים עוֹד

4.

I needed the body as well
to break
but it did not
crash
flocks of birds entered
the flesh
sparrows and bleeding wrens
sap seeping out of balsam trees
frozen as glass, shining
as a plastic scarf
under a moon thrown in the garbage
I ceased to see
how I shall live
life anymore
what of

ה.

וְלֹא יָדַעְתִּי שֶׁאֶצְטָרֵךְ לִחְיוֹת
אֶת מוֹתֵךְ, וְכַמָּה פָּשׁוּט יִהְיֶה לְנַסֵּחַ
אֶת זֶה. כְּמוֹ שֶׁאִמָּא
הַסְבִּירָה לַנְּכָדִים, לֹא נִרְאֶה
אֶת אֲבִיבָה עוֹד אַף פַּעַם. וְשָׁמַעְתִּי
אוֹתָהּ בּוֹכָה, לֹא הַקִּינָה
הַזֹּאת הַמְנֻחֶמֶת, רַק הַשֶּׁטֶף
שֶׁל מִי שֶׁכּוֹחוֹתָיו אָפְסוּ בַּלֶּהָבָה.
וְהֵם שָׁאֲלוּ תְּפוּסֵי תְּמִיהָה
אִם טִפַּסְתְּ לַכּוֹכָב, מָה
תַּעֲשִׂי אִם יִפֹּל, אִם תִּהְיִי רְעֵבָה.
וְהִיא הִנִּיחָה אוֹתָם בְּמִסְתּוֹר
הַקְּסָאם וּבָאָה יְפוּחָה אֶל
הַסָּלוֹן שָׁם יָשַׁבְתִּי
וּכְבָר אָמַרְתִּי
כַּמָּה פָּשׁוּט לִרְאוֹת אֶת זֶה
בַּחֲשֵׁכָה כְּמוֹ גַּחֶלֶת–
לְאַבֵּד יֶלֶד פֵּרוּשׁוֹ תָּמִיד לְאַבֵּד יֶלֶד.

5.

And I did not know that I would have to live
your death, and how easily
it would fit into words. Just as Mother
explained to the grandchildren, we will
never see Aviva again. And I heard
her cry, not that howling
lamentation, just the flow
of one whose strength vanished in the flame.
And they asked, caught up in wondering,
if you climbed up to a star, what
would you do if it fell, would you be hungry.
And she put them in the bomb
shelter and came sobbing to
the living room where I sat
and said
how simple it is to see
in the dark, like an ember glowing wild—
losing a child means always losing a child.

יא.

יְשׁוּעָה וּפַחַד הָיוּ לַצְנִינִים-
צִפּוֹר צָלְלָה בִּסְבַךְ עֵץ הַזַּיִת;
צִפּוֹר חָרְצָה קוֹל בַּגֶּשֶׁם.
גּוּפִי נַעֲנָה לַיְרֵשָׁה בְּהֹלֶם: אֶפְשָׁרֻיּוֹת
שֶׁל כְּאֵב, עַצְמוּתוֹ הַשְּׁפוּכָה
שֶׁל הַדָּם, חֵפֶץ-
לֵב שֶׁטָּבְעוּ אֲחֵרִים.

11.

Salvation and fear turned into thorns—
a bird shrieked in the olive tree thicket;
a bird chiseled sound in the rain.
My body succumbed to the inheritance, pulsing: possibilities
of pain, the spilt quiddity
of the blood, whole—
heartedness demanded by others.

טו.

הָבוּ לִי אֶת הַצּוּרוֹת הַמְצֵרוֹת אֶת הַשָּׂפָה
וַאֲפָרְקֵן אֵיבָר-אֵיבָר,
אֶעֱרֹן עַד הַיְּסוֹד, מַעֲלָלָן
אֶשְׁבֹּר אֶל סֶלַע,
שֶׁרְמוּטוֹת אֲיֻמּוֹת אוֹמְרוֹת אֲבִיבָה מֵתָה.
אֲבָל הָיִיתִי גַם
אֲנִי, דְּפָקָה עִבְרִית בְּתוֹךְ
גְּרוֹנִי, עָנִיתִי הֵן.
זֹאת זַיִן שֶׁל גָּמָל יֵשׁ לָהּ.

15.

Let me have those shapes that shrivel language
And I shall take them apart one-by-one,
I shall lay bare their roots,
their evil-doings I shall dash against the stone,
malicious sluts say Aviva is gone.
But there was I
as well, Hebrew pounding on
my throat-bell, I answered aye.
It has the dick of a camel, that one.

Born in Buenos Aires in 1963, Alejandra Laurencich has received numerous distinctions and awards, most notably the prestigious Segundo Premio Municipal for Historias de mujeres oscuras *(2007). She also founded* La Balandra, *a journal for beginning writers.*

Los dinosaurios no han muerto

Esa noche dejé el sillón del living en el que había estado tirado durante los últimos seis meses, salí de casa y tomé el primer taxi que se me cruzó. Tenía puesta una camisa planchada, doscientos mangos en el bolsillo interior del saco y la voluntad de cambiar algo, salir a ver qué pasaba en el mundo, apartarme de ese círculo de pensamientos que me llevaban a Mirna, a su decisión de abandonarme, a su frase predilecta: no te hagas ilusiones, ya nada puede cambiar.

—Anda para Barracas—le dije al taxista, seguro de que nunca me la encontraría a ella por ese barrio. No era un sitio que pudiera agradarle. Y mucho no se equivocaba. Cuando llegamos a esas calles desiertas, donde los únicos ejemplares de humanidad que parecían habitarlas eran dos tipos que fumaban sospechosamente en la puerta de un kiosco, examiné la posibilidad de dar la vuelta y volver al departamento. Todavía estoy a tiempo, me dije justo cuando el chofer me apuró:

—Ya estamos en Barracas, adónde lo llevo.

Vi un cartel de neón que decía *Night's Cupido* con una flecha hacia abajo y dije:

—Ahí en la puerta está bien.

Pagué y bajé. El taxi se perdió rápido en el empedrado. . . .

The Dinosaurs Have Not Died

That evening I got out of the recliner in the living room in which I had been lying for the last six months, left the house, and took the first taxi that crossed my path. I was wearing an ironed shirt, had two hundred pesos in the inside pocket of my jacket, and the inclination to change something, to go out and see what was happening in the world, to get away from that circle of thoughts that lead me to Mirna, her decision to abandon me, her favorite saying: don't kid yourself, nothing can change any more.

"Head toward Barracas," I told the driver, certain that I would never run into her in that neighborhood. It wasn't a place she would find pleasing. And she was absolutely right. When we got to those deserted streets, where the only signs of humanity that seemed to inhabit the place were two guys smoking suspiciously in the doorway of a kiosk, I considered the possibility of turning around and going back to the apartment. There's still time, I said to myself just as the driver announced, "We're in Barracas, where you asked me to bring you."

I saw a neon sign that said *Night's Cupid* with an arrow below it and said, "Over by that entrance is fine."

I paid and got out. The taxi took off fast on the cobblestone. I looked at the doorway to the dive. A stairway, whose bottom I could not see, lead downward. It was Good Friday but I was sure the place would look just as unexciting if it were a Sunday during Carnival.

Just as I started to go down the steps, the air thickened and became heavier as I proceeded. Maybe it was the smell: a strange mix of humidity, rat poison, and the deodorizer used in hotels for assignations. I was never one to have a fine sense of smell, but that stench seemed like a warning of something unhealthy. I stopped and thought that it would be better for me to get back to my recliner at home. But then I'd need to look for a taxi or the stop for some bus that would get me out of this cul-de-sac. The thought that the illusion of breaking my recent run of bad luck could end up in simple armed robbery depressed me too much. I went on down. The only thing more or less lit was the bar in the back of the tavern. I headed towards it, excusing myself with every step. I could make out couples who were dancing and others who were pulled up at the tables. And among all of them, or coming off of them, was that smell. *Of a hotel for assignations.* The phrase appeared to me as if written in the air. This has been happening to me lately. A sentence or some random word appears as if born of a thought (sometimes mine, sometimes someone else's) and starts to shimmer, about five inches in front of my forehead. And it won't leave me alone until I repeat it out loud two or three times, like an idiot, or until another replaces it. Horacio says it's because of the stress of the last few months, the loneliness, the anti-anxiety meds.

I sat down on a stool. The music was going *ta, ta, ta, ta.* Drums being played ineptly, without any enthusiasm. No one's voice stood out. *Hotel for assignations* kept shining there. The phrase, written on an invisible blackboard. With the uniform handwriting that I use for exam questions at the university. It was moving slowly and behind it I could see myself reflected in the mirror. Between a bottle of Seagram's whiskey and another of Old Smuggler. They made me want to order a drink, but I'd gotten out of the habit because of the meds. I didn't know how to start my night.

"Hotel for assignations," I repeated to myself. The writing began to fade. "Hotel for assignations," I said again as I looked at the prices on the sign. *Happy tour, Fridays after midnight.* Hour changed to tour. Any other warnings? Mirna would have gotten very angry if she'd seen me come into this place, I was sure of that. The certainty was making me feel guilty. A bit. Guilt is a comfortable state, the analyst Horacio recommended to me had said. Horacio had also recommended leaving my apartment, distracting myself.

Next to me at the bar was a woman with orange hair. I supposed that outside the bar and that dense penumbra her hair would look blond, light blond. Dyed. She was alone. Her elbows rested on the padded edge of the bar, and her chin was in her hands. She seemed to me to be asleep. In front of her a tall glass was nearly half full of a clear liquid. It wasn't water. I waited for the bartender to bring me the beer I'd ordered. Horacio said that to win women over you had to surprise them, not just start out with the usual silly things. What's your name and all that was for kids, for the students we were flunking daily at the university. Here, or in a disco, the lecturers like Horacio or like me, cool guys nearing fifty, were at a disadvantage.

She looked at me. She had pretty eyes, slanted and disarmingly transparent like Mirna's when she swam in the sea or took a shower, or when she had been crying. The woman's were lined too heavily in black for my taste, but they looked powerful, just the same. I took a sip of beer. She kept looking at me. Start off with something that's out there and you'll win for sure, Horacio always advised.

"I think that the dinosaurs have not died," was the first thing that occurred to me. Really out there, nonsense with a certain overtone of profundity due to the use of the present perfect. For a second I was proud of my idea, until the equation *dinosaur = old woman = error*, appeared in front of me; the phrase had replaced the other, the one about hotels, and I knew that repeating it to make it disappear would be to bury myself alive, but the woman with the orange hair, who wasn't exactly a dinosaur, said, while clenching her jaw as if she were fighting back the urge to punch someone: "And what the fuck do I care?"

Well, you sure screwed that up, I said to myself. I grabbed my beer and turned around on the stool, at such an angle that, in effect, I turned my back on my interlocutor, as if I were bringing the dialogue to a close. "Dinosaur, old woman, error. Dinosaur, old woman, error," I muttered. There were some people dancing, and others who were seated very close to each other, like Mirna and I were able to be sometimes. Ta, ta, ta. The music was beginning to bother me. The beer was freezing cold. There are pretty women in every bar, Horacio had said. I didn't see any.

"What did you come here for?" the voice coming over my shoulder sounded orange, like her hair.

And what the fuck does it matter to you, I felt like snapping back. It would have done me good to say it. But I turned towards her slowly, wondering if I would get used to the irritating way she spoke, as if she were letting words out between her clenched teeth. Nice tits.

"I beg your pardon?" I asked.

She stared at me. Without taking her big eyes off me she reached for her glass and took a less than innocent sip.

"Mineral water at this time of night?" I said to her.

She half closed her eyes and gave me a smirk. I thought that she was going to swear at me as she had before.

"A Belgian woman who died of cirrhosis of the liver used to call it jinja."

"Jinja?"

She looked at the glass then emptied it. She stared at me again.

"We call it gin here," she clarified, and I wasn't sure if *here* referred to the bar or to the country. Nor did I much care. I finished my beer and called the bartender.

"Two gins," I said without thinking. Mirna was probably grading exams, unwrapping a piece of candy with those long slender fingers of hers.

The orange-haired woman took out a pack of Lucky Strikes and asked if I'd like one. It was starting to work. I saw *This is how you proceed* form immediately. It seemed like Horacio's writing.

"This is how you proceed," I muttered.

"Wha?" she asked, in the same way kids imitate ducks. It wasn't the French *quoi*, not even a *what* that you would have pronounced unenthusiastically, just *wha*, plain and simple. It reminded me of my grandfather's characteristic *Oh?* that he used instead of the traditional *Huh?* that most folks would use when they don't understand what's being said to them. The waiter brought the two glasses of gin. I took a long drink. I looked at her; I was beginning to relax. The night was promising.

"Wha?" I said, without hiding my mockery. She didn't catch the reference, or it didn't perk her up.

"Yes. What did you just say?"

"You have nice skin."

"Thank you but don't be a fuckin' wiseass with me."

"Do you also eat with that mouth of yours?"

"And I can suck you off if I feel like it."

"Whoa!" I said. I put my hand over my crotch to control my erection, in case of trouble. I hadn't had sexual relations for a long time and imagining the orange-haired woman sucking me off had the effect of watching a porno film. I looked at myself in the mirror. But in the semidarkness I could only make out the letters of the sentence. *This is how you proceed*. She drank sensuously from her glass. No, she was no dinosaur. I figured that she must be about forty-five. I rested my hand against her back, at the neckline of her dark dress and I looked for the nape of her neck under the orange mane.

"This is how you proceed," I murmured.

She suddenly put down her glass. I lowered my hand.

"That again. What are you, a cop?"

"What?"

"You keep saying *proceed*."

She spoke with her mouth almost closed, that was it. As if she held an old grudge. Rage against humanity. I stared at her: not only did she have lovely skin, when she was quiet her lips relaxed. Beneath their sadness, her eyes became touching.

"Open that mouth," I said and I was already kissing her. The taste of gin was sweet on her breath. Her tongue slipped softly like a little eel. When we separated I had to catch my breath.

"And?" I said. "Do I still seem like a cop?"

"I never kissed one."

"Me neither," I said. The two of us laughed. *This is how you proceed* started to fade away on its own, without any effort on my part. That kind of miracle made me feel young, liberated. We drank and looked at one another again.

"What else have you not done in your life?" I asked, expecting that the answer would be black kissing or some such perversion.

"Finishing fourth grade," she said. I had to make an effort to understand what she was talking about.

The gin was beginning to take away the agility of my mental response but not my physical agility, which seemed to speed up faster than my willpower. My hand was lightly stroking her back. An illiterate, Mirna would have said, and it angered me to remember the types of categories she would establish without any scruples, as an expression of her style and superiority.

"My grandfather didn't get much schooling but he was a guy that people admired."

"That's nice."

"Yes." I got hung up on the adjective she used—nice. And the childish way she pronounced it.

She slowly exhaled smoke. I felt like telling her about my

grandfather. Don't go on, I said to myself, this isn't a therapy session.

"Do you know that story about someone who was born in an apple crate and dies in a gold coffin?" I said. The waiter had brought me more beer. I wondered who had ordered it. I poured a glass and began to drink. "Well, I don't know if it's a story, a joke, or just a saying. But it fits my grandfather just right."

"Does he have a gold coffin?"

I almost choked from laughing.

"No, no, nothing like that. He's not Tutankhamun," I said. She looked at me with a startled expression. "Tutankhamun, the Egyptian pharaoh. Oh, it doesn't matter. I'm talking about respect, about life, what do I know? When my grandfather died, his expression was peaceful, as if he were saying to us: I used to be this guy, now I'm done. I'm retiring. And he closed his eyes. Just like that."

"A privileged man."

She kept on talking, about men, I think, their way of looking or dying. I nodded my head, but I was distracted. I was thinking about the word with which she had defined someone like my grandfather. Privileged. It had never occurred to me to think about him as a privileged man. And it was true. Where had this woman come up with those definitions: nice, privileged. Words that contrasted with that rough way of talking. Syllables muttered between her teeth. For a second I imagined a dictionary on her night table, read devotedly. The interior of a miserable room, like Raskolnikov's in *Crime and Punishment*. The euphoria with which I had begun the conversation faded somewhat. I looked at her in the mirror. She was muttering something, thoughtfully, as if she found the story about my grandfather to be moving. As if it were about a daughter who just found out how her father died. It made me feel a bit naked. The mention of my grandfather had, I supposed, led me into complicated terrain. There was no longer any music going ta, ta, ta, like before. The place had gone silent. I had a strange sensation, of having been on a stage playing a role, while some tiny stagehands had been working to change scenes. The first act was over; the jokes were finished. Where am I? I wondered. I didn't want to keep on talking about my grandfather or anyone else. Something was going on behind me. I looked over my shoulder, certain of finding the place empty, that sinister semidarkness I'd crossed to get here, avoiding couples and tables, to end up where I was now sitting at the bar. What I saw calmed me down a bit: a small stage I hadn't noticed before was now lit with bluish spotlights. On it was a boy dressed in a red bullfighter's costume, adjusting a violin under his chin. I saw him enveloped in the dense cigarette smoke. A supernatural image. His dark, Indian skin, and that moth-eaten matador's costume he was wearing. He introduced himself as a Chilean and began to play some sad music.

She kept on talking, looking towards the mirror as she talked, as if confessing to herself.

"Most people have trouble saying goodbye. Whether they're twenty-five or seventy, they look like they're thinking *Hold on a second. Don't do it.*"

"Don't do what?" I asked, but she didn't hear me or didn't want to answer. She kept talking and looking at the mirror, into the depths of the mirror, as if she saw something behind it. "Don't do what?" I asked again, but the question was imperceptible, it was in my thoughts and in that phrase that was twinkling in front of me: *Don't do it.*

My temples were throbbing. The sound of the violin, piercing my soul. My thoughts were whirling at an incredible speed. She's talking about the ones who are going to die, you jerk, was one of those thoughts, one of those ideas that I noticed as it whizzed by without stopping, mixing with the nauseating smell and the letters of happy tour, and that suspicion of having landed in no man's land. Suddenly I sensed a void in my brain. My mind, empty now, focused on one single thought: she's talking about the ones who are going to die. It occurred to me that I was sitting next to a murderer. I reached for my drink and finished it off. I observed her out of the corner of my eye, looking for the detail that would betray her. She had her purse on her lap, not on the bar like other women, or hanging from her shoulder. On her lap. And there was a bulge in the bag. Illiterate and a murderer. Mirna again.

"Don't do it," I said.

She heard me.

"Yes, like that. It seems like they're telling you: 'Stop, give me a little time to tell you about it, I had dreams, I didn't want to end up this way.'"

Good night, nice meeting you. What are you waiting for in order to split? Get the hell out of here, I commanded myself. But the only thing moving were my hands rubbing my thighs as if I were massaging the back of an animal. She was looking at the mirror. Her gaze empty. Her jaws tense.

"Don't do it," I repeated and felt like a bigger idiot than usual. The sentence was going away but each time I said it my tone was more pitiful, it was becoming doglike, and she was throwing me more leftovers, with such clear anguish that it kept me at her side:

"Don't do it, yes. You feel like a jerk. You know you're taking away their last chance of receiving a kiss, or a hug from their family and that you have to do it. That's the way it is. You realize that some of them deserved a different life. But what are you going to do?"

"What are you going to do?" I repeated. I looked into her eyes.

"Nothing. You seal up the casket and that's the end of the story."

A hit of adrenaline made me bolt upright.

"What do you do?"

She brought the cigarette to her mouth, looking at me. She took a drag and blew the smoke into my face.

"Are you deaf? Or are you jerkin' me around?"

I was going to justify myself with some kind of excuse but she kept talking:

"I told you a little while ago. I seal caskets."

"Caskets."

"Yes, caskets," she said in a muffled voice. "With a soldering iron at the funeral home around the corner," she looked into the bottom of her glass. "A guy says to the relatives: If you want to say goodbye to the departed…And then I grab the soldering iron and that takes care of it."

We remained silent. Listening to the Chilean's violin. She felt far away, or so I tried to feel her, since I didn't want to get mixed up with her anguish, as if it were something she had earned. I was sorry I had told her about my grandfather. I regretted having ordered another round of gin. The bartender served them in front of us, filled to the brim, and when he finished, he winked at her, as if to say: Come on, you don't have far to go, you've almost got him. Being in this place began to make me uneasy. As if I were being infected by something. Though it wasn't exactly fear, but rather some kind of terrifying emotion, perhaps the demented euphoria of the damned. What was I doing there, next to that woman who was slowly drinking her gin and talking through her clenched jaw? On the stage, the Chilean was singing in a castrato's voice, something about a gypsy woman. Images from my life superimposed themselves in my memory. Walks with Mirna through the halls of the university, leaving the student assemblies. The smell of rosemary over the shed where my grandfather had his workshop. The angel hair soup that my mom served me when I got home from school. I remembered Agent 86, Maxwell Smart, when he said to his partner: Let's just pretend, 99.

"Did you *send off* many?"

Those beautiful eyes watched me, I supposed they were sizing up opportunity, or fear, as they must have done each time, with different corpses, before sealing the cover forever.

"I started when I was nineteen."

I looked back at the exit sign, among the couples and the smoke, the young guy in red was singing in a shaky voice and no one seemed to be paying any attention.

"And how did you happen to decide to devote yourself to that?"

She took a while to answer. When she did, she used the word necessity.

I could hear the voice of the castrato. *Since I don't know, tell me fortuneteller...if I'll survive this adventure alive or if I'll die.*

"You can always look for something else, right?" I said. But it was more of a plea than a certainty.

"Something else. What other fucking work would I know how to do?"

I grabbed her hand, not as a tender gesture. It was more like I was trying to immobilize her forever. She surrendered. She had delicate bones. I was going to tell her about illusions but I preferred to light a cigarette. The gypsy song was playing again and she looked at me. *Whether I'll lose my life in this adventure or triumph...*

"Don't you regret anything?" I said, with a harsh tone of superiority.

She lowered her gaze and held it on my glass. She moved her hand softly out from under mine.

"I was not happy," she said. She slid her thumb around the edge of the glass. I felt the urge to take off my blazer and put it over her shoulders. But I wasn't sure she was the one who was trembling.

"Everything is going to change," I said and for the first time I saw something like hope in her eyes. Her clear, immense eyes, behind the sentence that began to shine there, in Mirna's authoritative handwriting, Mirna's favorite sentence during the preceding months: *Nothing can change anymore.*

How to look at her through those condemning words? But in order to erase them I had to repeat them. And I wasn't going to do that. I couldn't. Even if that sentence danced all night between me and this woman. Fuck off, Mirna, I thought. And there was something heroic in me, something unknown that seemed to have awakened upon contact with this devastated woman. I could raise her hopes, show her that there was still time to become something other than a sealer of caskets. Maybe by saving her, I was saving myself.

A little tune played under her tits. She pulled away and rummaged in her purse. I caressed her hair. She looked at her cell phone and said, "I have to go to my fucking job."

I drank up what was left in my glass.

"It's just for a bit and then I'll be back," she excused herself, with sincerity. "If you wait for me, I'll be back in a half hour."

She got down from the stool without stumbling. I tried to do the same and could not. She was tall. I didn't want her to go.

"I'll take you in a cab," I begged.

"It's just around the corner."

I needed to gain some time and she was leaving.

"Tell me what your name is." She straightened her dress and did not answer. "My name is Ezequiel, please tell me your name." She smiled and put out her cigarette.

"Around here they call me Crow."

"Crow?" I said. She adjusted her purse. She was already leaving. "It's too harsh," I said.

She shrugged. "I'll seal a casket and be right back. Will you wait?"

I stared at the way she was leaving. The way her orange hair disappeared in the darkness. I imagined the spark of the soldering iron shining in her blue eyes. Her name had begun to form itself in print, like that from an old-fashioned book.

"What do I owe you?" I asked the bartender. I paid the tab and looked for the exit. The crystalline air of dawn made me shudder. As I wandered off I could see her name shining in front of me.

Søren Ulrik Thomsen's poetry, lauded as "more metamorphosis than metaphor," illuminates hidden corners in us all. One of Denmark's foremost living poets, Thomsen has written seven volumes of poems, four of essays, and one photo essay/paean to the vanishing funky areas of Copenhagen.

Den salte smag af dit kys kan jeg tydeligt huske
skønt den forsvandt for mange år siden,
en lille forviklet sekvens
af toner jeg fangede i farten
klirrer i skrivende stund i mit hoved;
men døden kender jeg kun fra frygten for den,
Guds ord fra oversættelser
og stilheden kun fra de lyde der høres
når man vågner en vinternat 05:30:
Bagtrappens knagen
        en tonstung lastvogns langsomme nedbremsen
et sted derude i mørket.

The salt taste of your kiss I remember clearly
though it vanished many years ago;
a small, intricate sequence
of notes caught in passing
rings in my mind as I write;
but death I know only from my fear of it,
God's word from translations
and silence only from the sounds heard
on wakening in winter blackness at 5:30 a.m.:
creak of the back stairs
        slow braking of a two-ton truck
somewhere out in the dark.

...kalenderen, hvor blyanten har understreget de dårlige datoer!
—Baudelaire

På de dårlige dage
hvor en hjemløs fortvivelse har fået asyl
og en flok krager på besøg fra middelalderen
stirrer på mig fra de høje bladløse træer
på de onde dage
hvor ord som Jezabel, napalm og Ritalin
lyder som en del af liturgien
og lyset styrter sammen
netop idet det når frem til mit vindue
på de spejlblanke dage
hvor bogstaverne i mine digte
letter med et ryk fra det hvide papir
og flyver bort som sorte insekter
på de ensomme dage
hvor jeg ikke kan huske min kærestes navn
men hvert eneste ansigt
jeg nogensinde har set i bussen
må jeg holde mig vågen til daggry
af frygt for drømmen
om det brændende diskotek.

...the calendar with its pencil rings round ominous dates!
—Baudelaire

On the bad days
where a homeless despair is granted asylum
and a flock of crows visiting from the middle ages
stares at me from tall leafless trees
on the evil days
where words like *Jezebel*, *napalm* and *Ritalin*
sound like part of the liturgy
and the light crashes apart
just as it reaches my window
on the mirror-slick days
where the letters in my poems
lift off with a shudder from the white paper
and fly away like black insects
on the lonely days
where I can't remember my girlfriend's name
but do remember every single face
I've ever seen on the bus
I have to stay awake till dawn
for fear of the dream
of the burning nightclub.

For hver gang vi sås
måske for at høre estisk musik

og kigge på fuglenes
små ufortolkelige skrifttegn i blæsten

var dit skelet styrtet lidt mere sammen
et sted derinde i frakken

men fordi blikket og stemmen
ja selv dine hænder

blev ved med at svæve

er det nu lige så umuligt
at tro du helt er forsvundet

som det dengang var svært at forstå
at du stadig gik rundt på Nørrebro

Every time we saw each other
maybe to listen to Estonian music

and watch the birds'
small indecipherable markings in the wind

your skeleton had collapsed a little farther
somewhere there inside your coat

but because your gaze and voice
and even your hands

stayed afloat in the air

it's now just as impossible
to believe you're completely gone

as it then was hard to understand
that you were still walking around Nørrebro.

Mellem alle disse digte
om døden og erindringen
er der her blevet plads til 11 linjer
om mælkebøtterne
hvis lys jeg igen i år havde glemt
med ét bliver tændt som et tivoli
og om at falde i hver sin søvn
i den samme seng
og vågne mens natten er dybest
og stilheden størst
med en hånd så let på sin skulder.

Among all these poems
about death and memories
there's still room for 11 lines
about dandelions
whose light I had again this year forgotten
switches on all at once like a carnival
and about us, each falling into our own sleep
in the same bed
and wakening when night is deepest
and silence greatest
with a hand laid so lightly over our shoulders.

31 december.
Jeg tager motorvejen ud til kysten
hvor et gråkoldt hav
kaster uigenkendelige genstande op på stranden.
Et par tanker er helt tænkt til ende
andre svæver som en opskræmt allikeflok
over den blændende snemark.
På vej tilbage over parkeringspladsen
standser jeg pludselig op.
Men lyden af mine skridt
fortsætter ind under tågen.

December 31st.
I take the highway out to the coast
where a graycold sea
flings unrecognizable things ashore.
A couple of thoughts are thought through
others float like a flock of startled jackdaws
over the glaring field of snow.
On the way back across the parking lot
I suddenly stop.
But the sound of my footsteps
goes on, into the fog.

"A Wash of Mimicry": On the Deformation Zone of Translation

1.

Poetry is what gets lost in translation.

I'm fond of pointing out that one of the most canonical definitions of poetry in America relies on translation. This suggests that translation—even if through negation—is *essential* to the American concept of poetry. We define poetry through translation, its opposite.

It might be strange to assert the prominence of translation in an age when we know—thanks to the work of critics and activists like Lawrence Venuti, Chad Post, Don Mee Choi, and Lucas Klein—that the translator and her translations are "invisible": marginal, debased. But somehow the translator and translation are simultaneously marginal and central, both invisible and hyper-visible—if only as a threat, a ghost, kitsch.

If we want to find out why translation is in such fundamental opposition to poetry, we might ask ourselves: What *is* this something that's "lost" in translation?

The short answer: the singular poem, the singular author writing within a single, patriarchal lineage. In other words: the illusion of a perfect, well-wrought urn of a text that can't be paraphrased—or rather that isn't paraphrased—written by one original author who expresses his or her views with absolute control of language.

But in translation we lose the illusion of a single lineage, and the supposed objectivity of that lineage. What if we don't actually know who is influencing who? What if a writer is influenced by a text that is alien to her—can she really be influenced "correctly"? Is she misreading? The threat of translation to poetry is the threat of excess: too many versions of too many texts by too many authors from too many lineages. Poetry, it appears, gets lost in a noisy, violent excess.

2.

Over the past two hundred years, many Western (not just American, if I'm perfectly honest) theorists have discussed the excess produced by translation in terms of a violence. In Walter Benjamin's classic essay "The Task of the Translator," this excess becomes a violent alienness within the text itself:

> If in the original, content and language constitute a certain unity, like that between a fruit and its skin, a translation surrounds its content, as if with the broad folds of a royal mantle. For translation indicates a higher language than its own and thereby remains inadequate, violent, and alien with respect to its content.[1]

In this metaphor the act of translation surrounds the skin with foreign clothes—an excess that makes the text no longer organic or in balance with itself. Translation seems not to be a lack (what is lost) but an accumulation—an infection by the alien. An alienness that is violent in part *because* it is alien, like a disease.

3.

The violence of translation is even more central to George Steiner's canonical study of translation, *After Babel*. Steiner portrays translating itself as a violent act: the translator must, in an act of "aggression" and "penetration," "extract" the meaning (as if it were gold in some colonial enterprise). However, the translator must take care not to lose her sense of self as she incorporates the new text into the target culture. Steiner warns that translating might—like a sexual intercourse—lead to "infection": "No language, no traditional symbolic set or cultural ensemble imports without the risk of being transformed." Here, though, the infection is not only that of the text, but of the target culture; the transformative infection may ruin our sense of self: "We may be mastered and made lame by what we have imported."

Steiner asserts that the infection problem posed by translation is one of economics.[2] Not only must the translator be aware not to lose him or herself, but the greater culture has to incorporate the translation into its own context and literary lineage in order to avoid "inflation." If this is not avoided, the target literary culture might "generate...a wash of mimicry."[3] "Fidelity," Steiner argues, "is ethical, but also, in the full sense, economic." The translator must create "a condition of significant exchange...ideally, exchange without loss."[4] The threat of translation is that it might produce an excess that would ruin the economy of meaning.

4.

Through political and economic power that makes the U.S. central and the rest of the world peripheral, we have guarded our literature well from this "mimicry flood." So deeply entrenched and unthinking is our opposition to translation that even translators and translation critics seem to believe in the impossibility of translation. Even Lawrence Venuti himself—one of the most influential translation activists and critics of the past 20 years—aligns himself with the impossibility of translation. Even as he calls for better contractual terms and more "visibility" for the translator, Venuti repeats that translation is impossible. The most important reason why Venuti sees it as impossible is because the "original context" is lost:

>...a reader of a translation can never experience it with a response
>that is equivalent or even comparable to the response with which
>the source-language reader experiences the source text, that is to say
>a reader who has read widely in the source language and is immersed
>in the source culture. Not even a bilingual reader familiar with both
>the source and the translating cultures will experience the two texts
>in the same or a similar way.[5]

Throughout his work, Venuti insists on an original "context" with
an original reader, an "educated" native reader who fully appreciates
the text through her mastery of the context. This model is frequently
repeated in translation discussions: the successful translator is a foreigner who has gained mastery of the source culture, a mastery often
illustrated by attention to cultural differences (for example, Venuti
finds flaw with a Calvino translator for translating *ricotta* as "cream
cheese"). Although Venuti allows for Derrida's idea of "iterability,"
he insists that an original text is stabilized by an original reader and
context.[6]

The good translation for Venuti is a translation that *reveals* that
context is lost, a translation that informs, that does not try to fool us.
A good translation reminds us that there is another world out there
that is not ours. This is the idea of the "foreignizing translation," a
translation that through linguistic noise calls attention to its status
as a translation: "The point is rather to develop a theory and practice
of translation that resists dominant target-language cultural values
so as to signify the linguistic and cultural difference of the foreign
text."[7] It doesn't fool you into thinking it's poetry; it doesn't absorb
but distances.

Venuti posits this translation model as opposed to the "domesticating" practice that attempted to make the foreign seem American by
smoothing out translation noise. But, paradoxically, in so doing he still
prescribes a way of presenting the foreign text (thus domesticating it)

and makes our experience instrumental to the text.[8] The foreign text is forced to serve a definite purpose: to remind Americans that there is a foreign world out there. Venuti writes: "Foreignizing translation signifies the difference of the foreign text, yet only by disrupting the cultural codes that prevail in the target language...deviating enough from the native norms to stage an alien reading experience..."[9] In Venuti's theory, translation's inflationary threat to the target culture is merely readjusted to serve a specific purpose: revealing its own ghostly threat.

Both "domesticating" and "foreignizing" translation models (and virtually every talk or discussion about translation I've ever read or witnessed) depend on context as a stabilizing model. But what is "context"? In Venuti's essays, the "original context" is equated with how an "educated reader" in the "original culture" would have originally read the original poem. Lots of originals there and also a lot of presumptions: What is an "educated reader"? Is there only one way to be educated? What if the poet was uneducated? What if the poet was a foreigner? What if the poet's aesthetics were influenced by foreign literature? What if the poet—as often is the case—lived for a time in a foreign country? And can't we be foreign to ourselves? Poetry—and in particular poetry in translation—destabilizes notions of a stable context and authorship. We "lose" ourselves, we become "lame," in Steiner's words. Poetry is itself inflation. It teems.

5.

For Venuti, the violence of translation comes when removing a poem from its original context, but I agree with Steiner that there is a violence in how we are affected by translations (and even language, communication): We come undone, our selves are corrupted, infected, and even "shattered" (as Leo Bersani has put it).[10] Just as the translator enacts a type of violence on the foreign text, the text enacts violence on the translator. And I might add: just as a reader enacts violence against a poem, so the poem enacts violence on the reader. The recipient of any artwork is in danger of being infected, of being made part of the artwork, or even of having the top of their head taken off. And when that happens, writers who are the readers of these texts may indeed channel foreign writers, overflowing our own literature with "mimicry." A single lineage and hierarchy is troubled by writing that is "mimicry," i.e., overwhelmed instead of original, having abandoned its true self. But I don't think this is something we should seek to balance or stabilize.

To me, Georges Bataille's theories of excess provide an important alternative view of the urge for a balanced economy, an alternative Daniel Tiffany has called "the extravagant economy of the impossible."[11] Bataille argued there are two economies, one based on use and one based on waste—a "restricted" economy and a "general" economy, "represented by so-called unproductive expenditures: luxury, mourning, war, cults, the constructions of sumptuary monuments, games, spectacles, arts, perverse sexual activity…these represent the activities which, at least in primitive circumstances, have no end beyond themselves."[12] Bataille sees in the wasteful luxury of the nonproductive economy a rejection of capitalism. Poetry is on the side of loss, inflation, waste, excess.

6.

One of the most important contemporary poets is the Korean Kim Hyesoon. I know of her work through the translations of Korean-born translator, poet, and activist Don Mee Choi. I don't know "the original." I don't even know the Korean alphabet; my knowledge of a South Korean context is highly suspect at best. According to academic conventions, I can't know that she's a very important poet because I can't read her in the original. Venuti might object that in calling her important from my context I'm domesticating her by treating her as if she were an American poet, as if I had "access" to her work. I am supposed to quarantine her poetry.

But I don't want to. I want to say she is one of the most important contemporary poets, and that she is that—at least for me—through translation. We need not know the context in order to read a poem; to stabilize the poem in order to determine import. A poem brings its context with it and channels it to the reader. In her pig poems, Kim Hyesoon pulls me into the Korean meat horrors, but also into the identity of South Korea as an American colony:

> It's Pig, Pig who has never seen the outside, always Pig, depressed Pig, Pig who cries wolf, Pig who has chosen the most terrified pig in the world to be the king, Pig who shouts Oh, fantastic sewer! while hugging its pillow, Pig who laughs alone hoping mommy will get arrested, mommy who gave birth to Pig who will pig out till it drops dead, Pig with bloated lips who thinks the whole world is rice porridge, its XXXL Pig, Pig who takes up the entire bed, its name can only be Pig, shivering-shivering Pig whenever it hears Cross the ocean, yes-yes Pig who has never once raised its head, Pig who pigs out from fear when it looks up at the vast night sky, Pig who pigs out thinking that Pig who pigs out is Pig...[13]

In "Pig Pigs Out," Hyesoon's pigs proliferate, swarming the poem. The poem invokes not just the mass-slaughter of animals and the slaughterous aspect of global trade and military action that reduce *us* to pigs. But the sheer mass of the pigs, the excess of pig bodies also taps into a fear of proliferation—of translation, of art—that this essay has discussed: there is not just one "Pig," or one "Johannes," or one "Kim Hyesoon," but a teeming of Pigs. Every time one "Pig" is asserted, it seems to generate another one.

I respond to this visceral and grotesque imagery; I am moved by the frantic energy that drags me into its sewers and into the sewers of American colonialism and globalist modernity. I may be appropriating the text—absorbing or being absorbed by it. But along the way, I have been brought into a South Korean cultural—if not context, then—dynamic of repression and colony. And does a colony count as having an "original context"? Or is the context as Hyesoon said in a recent interview with *Guernica*, "put[ting] the disease of this world and my sick body together."[14]

7.

Note: This doesn't mean I want to act like there are no cultural differences, or that there is no violence in translations across national and linguistic borders. It hurts like hell.

8.

I recently translated the work of another great contemporary poet—Swedish poet Aase Berg's science fiction masterpiece *Dark Matter*, a dense hallucinatory book full of neologisms and collaged texts with an overall structure that rewrites Nobel laureate Harry Martinson's book *Aniara*:

> a) The bedrock wrenches its mass and ends up in the right notch. Continental plates topple and are cleft. Come Leatherface, my love, glide into the face of the secret's bestial longing. Feel the surface contact that boils shakes hard beneath the fragile grain-boundaryskin. Come, Golem simmers beneath the crawlanimals of our hands' bodies. At the leather-shedding of exposed humanoids. Glide into the heavy tunnel material of the kiss.[15]

It's a fascinating poem and a fascinating translation project, in large part because it is a text that deploys a wide range of words—taken from such sources as science and B movies—into a Swedish that is not an expert Swedish. It's a Swedish that fails to cohere; a Swedish best read perhaps not by an "educated reader" of Swedish, but by a foreigner, someone with an incomplete knowledge of Swedish.

Berg collages in technical terms like *bedrock*, *continental plates*, and *grain boundary* from geology but her poem is not a scientific text: one might say she finds the peel of scientific discourse, amplifying it and thus generating "a wash of mimicry." She jams the highly technical, abstract "grain boundary" together with "skin," as if to drag its meaning bodily into the visceral imagery. And by forging this neologism, she makes me see the term *kräldjur*, the standard word for "reptiles" in a new way: it consists of the two words *kraal* ("crawl") and *djur* ("animal"). Berg's poetry asks me to read it not as an educated reader but as a stranger to Swedish, a nonfluent, myopic reader. So I translate it as "crawl animals." It's a bad translation. It's impossible.

9.

I'm not a model translator: Not an American expert who travels to Sweden with a complete mastery over the English language and an extensive knowledge of the Swedish cultural context. I'm a Swedish immigrant; I don't write in my mother tongue, I translate it. But then Berg is not a model poet: she wrote *Dark Matter* while living in Amsterdam and trying to destroy her own ideas about poetry and also to get away from Sweden and its cultural climate. What is her cultural context? What is my cultural context? What is the context of expatriates? A poet who uses words she doesn't understand from contexts to which she is alien? A poet who is writing already awash in mimicry?

10.

Art is continually making and remaking itself, infecting and being infected by recipients and artists and writers and translators that may or may not have "access" to the foreign language text. The translation is not a separate, autonomous text—but then no texts are. Authors are not absolutely original originators. This is a scandal not just of translation but of art itself. Art creates what my wife Joyelle McSweeney and I have—stealing the term *deformation zone* from the title of an Aase Berg poem:

> …"acts of translation" are matters of one medium entering another's space, of one body saturating another, of disintegration, a disorientation of borders. As with a Kara Walker silhouette, a Möbius strip, or a great libidinous band (film), this new continuousness, this total contact is impossible, yet slavishness makes it, it gums up our ability to really know where anything starts and stops. It's a temporal send-up, a parody. It touches and slicks everything, breaks everything down…[16]

Art carries its (multiple, shifting, volatile) contexts into the deformation zone. It can't be fully determined by an illusion of a stable context, and the translator and reader have to venture into the zone as well. We have to catch its disease, be infected by it.

NOTES

1. Lawrence Venuti, ed., "The Task of the Translator," *The Translation Studies Reader* (New York: Routledge, 2012), 79.
2. In *Radio Corpse*, Daniel Tiffany brings in economics as well, suggesting the close connection between translation and Marx's idea of the "fetish."
3. George Steiner, *After Babel: Aspects of Language and Translation* (Oxford: Oxford University Press, 1998), 315.
4. Steiner, *Babel*, 318.
5. Lawrence Venuti, *Translation Changes Everything: Theory and Practice* (New York: Routledge, 2013), 180.
6. In this regard, his criticism has much in common with the "new historicist" readings that were so popular in the American academy in the 1990s.

7. Lawrence Venuti, *The Translator's Invisibility: A History of Translation* (New York: Routledge, 2008), 23.

8. I might even argue that he is radically domesticating, demanding that the translations work according to a model of "noisiness" that is very much based on an aesthetic institutionalized in the U.S. in the 1990s when Venuti began to publish his translation theories. Venuti's theory wants translations to function like language poems. Adding a complex layer to this context is the fact that language poets themselves have often referred to their works metaphorically as works in translation, or works that cannot be translated. In other words, they derive their politics from acting like foreign texts.

9. Venuti, *The Translator's Invisibility*, 20.

10. Leo Bersani, *The Culture of Redemption* (Cambridge, MA: Harvard University Press, 1992).

11. "Yet the impossible, as Georges Bataille observes, overwhelms utility, truth, and meaning, and thus engenders through translation unspeakable (and inconceivable) forms of exchange. Indeed, the impossibility lodged within translation is itself death, madness—and originality." (Tiffany, *Radio Corpse*, 187.)

12. Georges Bataille, "The Notion of Expenditure," *Visions of Excess: Selected Writings 1927–1939* (Minneapolis: University of Minnesota Press, 1985), 118.

13. Kim Hyesoon, "Pigs Pig Out," *Sorrowtoothpaste Mirrorcream*, trans. Don Mee Choi (Notre Dame, IN: Action Books, 2014), 75.

14. Kim Hyesoon (with Ruth Williams), "The Female Grotesque," http://www.guernicamag.com/interviews/williams_kim_1_1_12/

15. Aase Berg, "4.5 in Reactor," *Dark Matter*, trans. Johannes Göransson (Chicago: Black Ocean, 2012), 53.

16. Johannes Göransson and Joyelle McSweeney, *Deformation Zone* (New York: Ugly Duckling Presse, 2010).

Swiss poet Pierre Chappuis was born in 1930. Like his contemporaries Phillippe Jaccottet, Yves Bonnefoy, and André du Bouchet, Chappuis is an outstanding French-language poet interested in nature, metaphysics, and phenomenology.

Ces brassées d'étincelles, ces braises

Les coquelicots, encore—niant la solitude, traces d'un incendie prêt à reprendre, papillons aux ailes repliées qu'agite, vraie folie de parler inassouvie, le moindre vent venu de la mer.

Ensemble pour une fois (*impossible*) en pleins champs où tant de sépultures furent creusées: salut, sur nos lèvres insouciantes, à ces brassées d'étincelles, ces braises éparses parmi les herbes sèches!

Si proches alors nos bouches, elles-mêmes enflammées…

À l'espace (*l'azur, jusqu'à la transparence*), à tout l'espace vivifié de juillet (*ses ocres souterrainement répercutées*), avoir part, pleinement.

Autour d'eux un instant assis côte à côte à l'abri de la chaleur, entre eux (*si proches furent-ils*), pour eux seuls scintille le présent tandis que la stridence des hirondelles cisaille l'air au-dessus de leurs têtes.

Au fond des hypogées, des oiseaux également—couleur, leur vol! couleur, leur unique chant!—traversent la nuit.

These Armfuls of Sparks, These Embers

Poppies, again—denying solitude, traces of a fire about to flare up again, butterflies with folded wings, with their true craze for speaking left unappeased, stirred by the slightest wind coming from the sea.

Together for once (*impossible*) in the middle of fields where so many sepulchers were dug: a greeting, on our carefree lips, to these armfuls of sparks, these scattered embers among the dry grasses!

So close our mouths were then, also ablaze…

To have a full share of space (*the azure, all the way to transparency*), of all space livened by July (*its ocher hues reflected back underground*).

Around them for an instant as they are sitting side by side sheltered from the heat, between them (*no matter how close they were*), for them alone sparkles the present while the stridency of the swallows scissors the air above their heads.

At the bottom of the hypogea, birds as well—color, their flight! color, their one song!—traverse the night.

Ici, renouveau.

Éphémère, telle une traînée de poudre, tel un flot de paroles à venir, la même ocre, secrètement, le même frémissement pourpre (*leur jeunesse, à jamais*) trouble leur cœur.

Si proches (*impossible*) pour l'instant. Qu'ils le soient. Qu'ils le demeurent…

❖

À d'autres, leur tour venu, heureux, riches soudain d'un si lointain passé, à d'autres de suivre passagèrement, comme leurs propres traces, ces pointillés parmi les herbes dans le suspens du jour, écarlates au-dessus des tombes vides.

…Inaccompli sur le moment déjà, brûlant.

Here, renewal.

Ephemeral, like a powder trail, like a flood of words to come, the same ocher, secretly, the same purple trembling (*their youth, forever*) troubles their heart.

So close (*impossible*) for the moment. May they be so. May they remain so.

✤

It's up to others, their time now come, happy, suddenly enriched by such a remote past, up to others to follow for a while, as if it were their own tracks, this line of dots among the grasses in the suspense of the day, scarlet above empty graves.

…At this very moment already unaccomplished, burning.

Démarcation de l'incertain

Pour quel partage, cette ligne à peine tracée, droite, qui ne dévie pas, ce coup de ciseaux donné à l'aveugle par une main sûre?

Lac, brume; de déchirure, aucune.

Peut-être ne fut aucun voilier. Peut-être n'eut pas lieu.

Demarcation of the Uncertain

For what sharing this barely drawn, straight, never-veering line, this blind scissor cut given by a sure hand?

Lake, haze; any tearing?—none.

Perhaps no sailboat was. Perhaps did not happen.

Sur le qui-vive

Parmi ces feuilles mortes qu'il remue (*tête et bec*), qu'il pique, secoue, qu'il déchire, qu'il retourne pour les écarter aussitôt, les rejetant quelquefois par paquets, cet impatient (*fébriles, merle, tes coups de bec!*), cet affairé toujours sur le qui-vive, que cherche-t-il?

Quelle phrase? quelle version antérieure d'un poème (*le poème*), d'un rêve (*le rêve*) étourdiment mise de côté, perdue, noyée dans la masse d'innombrables brouillons, peut-être jamais écrite?

À force de variantes, de redites, il en vient à la croire, après tant et tant d'infructueux essais (*tout ce tintouin, cet embrouillamini de feuilles mortes*), il l'imagine à la fin (*renoncera-t-il?*) seule digne d'être retenue quand, justement, elle demeure introuvable.

On the Alert

Among the dead leaves that it stirs (*head and beak*), that it stabs, shakes, that it rips, that it turns over and pushes aside just as soon, rejecting sometimes whole little piles of them, what is this impatient one (*how feverish, blackbird, every jab of your beak!*), this busy one, ever on the alert, looking for?

What sentence? What former version of a poem (*the poem*), of a dream (*the dream*), carelessly put aside, lost, submerged among countless other drafts, perhaps never written?

By dint of variants, needless repetitions, he begins to believe in it, after so many fruitless attempts (*all this bother, this muddle-jumble of dead leaves*), he imagines it as ultimately being (*will he give up?*) the only one worthy of being kept, when, for that very reason, it cannot be found.

Rafael Courtoisie Beyhaut is one of Uruguay's leading writers. The internationally-published author of nineteen books and many essays has won Uruguay's national prize in both narrative and poetry. He teaches screenwriting at the Escuela de Cine del Uruguay in Montevideo.

El café

"Aceite funéreo",
lo llamó César Vallejo.
Sin embargo el café es una parte de la noche
la parte más despierta, la que se aleja del sueño
la parte tenebrosa.
Leche negra, el café, leche de sombra, alimento de monstruos
vino absurdo del otoño
agua del odio.
Para estar despierto, para vigilar, para matarse
el café.
Líquido negro.
En el alma no hay lugar para la dicha.
Se toma el café, su vigilia erecta
su ronca voz
su corazón negro.
Se toma el café, su eficiencia.
Una taza de café, un pocillo
un sorbo.
Se toma el café. Una dosis.
El café. Un poco.

Coffee

César Vallejo once called it
"Funereal oil."
But coffee is a part of the night
the most wakeful part, the part that steals away from sleep
the sinister part.
Black milk, coffee, shadow's milk, food for monsters
absurd wine of autumn
water of hatred.
To stay alert, to stay vigilant, to kill yourself
coffee.
Black liquid.
In its soul there is no room for joy.
Drinking coffee, its erect vigil
its hoarse voice
its black heart.
Drinking coffee, its efficiency.
A cup of coffee, a demitasse
a swallow.
Drinking coffee. One dose.
Coffee. Just a little.

A la mañana, el grito del café, su grito oscuro
a la mañana,
cuando hay que despertarse
el grito del café
un gallo líquido.
Su canto negro.

Coffee's cry to the morning, its dark cry
to the morning,
when you have to wake up
coffee's cry
a liquid rooster.
Its black song.

Las naranjas

Putas redondas, pelotas
llenas de hambre sexual, de una luz sometida
sin tiempo, de una vida agridulce
de la pasión idiota
de unos pocos momentos, del amor de un minuto
de la sombra, del sexo de los gajos
de la cáscara.
No se parecen al sol, no son como la luna
se parecen al atardecer, se parecen al viento
cuando sopla sobre las rocas, cuando habla el silencio.
Tienen una virtud: son locas.
La frescura y el dolor se parecen.
Las naranjas dementes no tienen pelo, no tienen voz
no tienen sentimientos.
Las naranjas son frescas, locas y frescas
como el jugo del pensamiento.

Oranges

Round whores, balls
full of sexual hunger, of a beaten light
outside time, of a bittersweet life
of idiotic passion
of a few short moments, of minute-long love
of shade, of the segments' sex
of the peel.
They don't look like the sun, aren't like the moon
they look like dusk, they look like the wind
when it blows over rocks, when silence speaks.
They possess a virtue: they're mad.
Freshness and pain look alike.
The demented oranges have no hair, have no voice,
have no feelings.
The oranges are fresh, mad and fresh
like thought juice.

La cuchara

La cuchara es la fruta más extraña del mundo. No se come. Sin embargo se lleva a la boca, tiene cáscara y es como la ilusión, dura y violenta.

La cuchara se mete en la sopa y la asusta. Se mete en el arroz y lo hiere, se mete en la harina y la muerde.

Sin embargo, no tiene dientes.

La cuchara no expresa sus sentimientos, es como el corazón de Dios, que está dormido y alegre, que no se mueve, que es duro pero se puede tocar, que no siente.

La cuchara no siente. El frío y el calor no la molestan.

Es necesaria sí, para la vida del hombre, pero también es rara.

Tanto, que no tiene temor de las estrellas, ni de las moscas, ni del tiempo eterno.

La cuchara vive sin saberlo, entre los otros cubiertos, al lado de los cuchillos filosos y de los tenedores ciegos, al lado de las tazas frías y junto a las papas violentas. Las cucharas se burlan del aceite.

Las cucharas son mujeres sin cuerpo, mujeres sin sentido, mujeres sin tiempo. Herramientas poderosas de un sutil recuerdo, de una mirada fugaz, de la voz de los muertos.

The Spoon

The spoon is the strangest fruit in the world. You don't eat it. However, you raise it to your mouth, it has a shell and it's like illusion, hard and violent.

The spoon gets into the soup and scares it. It gets into the rice and wounds it, gets into the flour and bites it.
But it doesn't have teeth.

The spoon doesn't express its feelings, it's like the heart of God, which is sleeping and happy, which doesn't move, which is hard but can be touched, though not feel.
The spoon doesn't feel. Cold and heat don't bother it.
It's necessary, for the life of man, but it's also rare.
So much so that it fears no stars, nor flies, nor time eternal.

The spoon lives without knowing it, amidst the rest of the cutlery, next to the sharp-edged knives and the blind forks, next to the cold glasses and alongside the violent potatoes. The spoons make fun of the cooking oil.

Spoons are women without bodies, women without sense, women without time. Powerful tools of a subtle memory, of a fleeting glance, of the voice of the dead.

Las cucharas llevan la voz de los muertos en el té, en el caldo. Las cucharas recuerdan. Y no tienen miedo.

Si ves una cuchara, sigue de largo. Piensa en la luna que vive feliz y blanca sin cucharas que la molesten.

Una cuchara es como el metal del silencio, dura y terrible, sin dueño.

Spoons carry the voice of the dead into tea, into broth. Spoons remember. And they are not afraid.

If you see a spoon, keep your distance. Think about the moon living happy and white without spoons to bother it.

A spoon is like the metal of silence, hard and terrible, without owner.

Disquiet sourced in a complex, tragicomic relation to time shows up in all of Antonio Tabucchi's work. This disquiet is expressed most intensely in Time Ages in a Hurry. *Tabucchi's work testifies masterfully to the imagination as time's worthiest interlocutor.*

Controtempo

Era stato cosí:

l'uomo si era imbarcato da un aeroporto italiano, perché tutto cominciava in Italia, e che fosse Milano o Roma era secondario, l'importante è che fosse un aeroporto italiano che permetteva di prendere un volo diretto per Atene, e da lì, dopo una breve sosta, una coincidenza per Creta con l'Aegean Airlines, perché di questo era certo, che l'uomo aveva viaggiato con l'Aegean Airlines, dunque aveva preso in Italia un aereo che gli dava una coincidenza da Atene per Creta intorno alle due del pomeriggio, lo aveva visto sull'orario della compagnia greca, il che significava che costui era arrivato a Creta intorno alle tre, tre e mezza del pomeriggio. L'aeroporto di partenza ha comunque un'importanza relativa nella storia di colui che aveva vissuto quella storia, è un mattino di una qualsiasi giornata di fine aprile del duemilaotto, una giornata splendida, quasi estiva. Il che non è un particolare insignificante, perché l'uomo che stava per prendere l'aereo, meticoloso com'era, dava molta importanza al tempo e seguiva un canale satellitare dedicato alla meteorologia di tutto il globo, e il tempo, aveva visto, a Creta era davvero splendido: ventinove gradi diurni, cielo sgombro, umidità nei limiti consentiti, un tempo da mare, l'ideale per stendersi su una di quelle spiagge bianche che ...

Against Time

It'd been like this:

the man had boarded at an Italian airport, because everything began in Italy, and whether it was Milan or Rome was secondary, what matters is that it was an Italian airport from which one could take a direct flight to Athens, and from there, after a brief stopover, a connecting flight to Crete on Aegean Airlines, because this he was sure of, that the man had traveled on Aegean Airlines, so in Italy he'd taken a flight that let him connect in Athens for Crete at around two in the afternoon, he'd seen it on the Greek company's schedule, which meant this man had arrived in Crete at around three, three-thirty in the afternoon. The airport of departure is not so important, though, in the story of the person who'd lived that story, it's the morning of any day at the end of April of two-thousand eight, a splendid day, like summer. Which is not an insignificant detail, because the man taking the flight, meticulous as he was, gave considerable importance to the weather and would watch a satellite channel dedicated to meteorology around the world, and the weather in Crete, he'd seen, was really splendid: twenty-nine degrees Celsius during the day, clear sky, humidity within normal limits, good seaside weather, ideal for lying on one of those white beaches described in his guide, for bathing in the blue sea and enjoying a well-deserved vacation. Because this was also the reason for the journey of that man who was going to live that story: a vacation. And in fact that's what he thought, sitting in the waiting lounge for international flights at Rome-Fiumicino, waiting for the loudspeaker to announce boarding for Athens.

And here he is finally on the plane, comfortably installed in business class—it's a paid trip, as will be seen later—reassured by the courtesies of the flight attendants. His age is difficult to define, even for the person who knew the story that the man was living: let's say he was between fifty and sixty years old, lean, robust, healthy-looking, salt-and-pepper hair, fine blond mustache, plastic glasses for farsightedness hung from his neck. His work. On this point too the person who knew his story was somewhat certain. He could be a manager of a multinational, one of those anonymous businessmen who spend their lives in an office and whose merit is one day acknowledged by headquarters. But he could also be a marine biologist, one of those researchers who by observing seaweeds and microorganisms under a microscope, without leaving their laboratory, are able to assert that the Mediterranean will become a tropical sea, as perhaps it was millions of years ago. Yet this hypothesis too struck him as not very satisfying, biologists who study the sea don't always remain shut up in their laboratory, they wander beaches and rocks, perhaps they dive, they perform their own surveys, and that passenger dozing in his business-class seat on a flight to Athens didn't actually look like a marine biologist, maybe on weekends he went to the gym and kept his own body in good shape, nothing else. But if he really did go to the gym, then why did he go? To what end did he maintain his body, so young-looking? There really was no reason: it'd been over for quite a while with the woman he'd considered his life companion, he didn't have another companion or lover, he lived alone, stayed away from serious commitments, apart from some rare adventures that can happen to everybody. Perhaps the most credible hypothesis was that he was a naturalist, a modern follower of Linnaeus, and he was going to a convention in Crete along with other experts on medicinal herbs and plants, abundant in Crete. Because one thing was certain, he was going to a convention of fellow researchers, his was a journey that rewarded a lifetime of work and commitment, the convention was taking place in the city of Retimno, he'd be put up in a hotel made of bungalows a few kilometers from Retimno, where a service car would take him in the afternoons, and he'd have mornings to himself.

The man woke up, pulled out his guide from his carry-on, and looked for his hotel. What he found was reassuring: two restaurants, a pool, room service, the hotel had closed during the winter and had reopened only in mid-April, and this meant very few tourists would be there, the usual clients, the Northern Europeans thirsty for sunlight as the guide described them, were still in their little boreal houses. The pleasant voice from the loudspeaker asked everyone to buckle their seat belts, they'd begun the descent to Athens where they'd land in about twenty minutes. The man closed the small folding table and put his seat upright, replaced the guide in his carry-on, and from the pocket of the seat in front of him pulled out the newspaper that the stewardess had distributed, to which he'd paid no attention. It was a newspaper with many full-color supplements, as is now common on weekends, the economics-financial one, the sports one, the interior-design one, and the magazine. He skipped all the supplements and opened the magazine. On the cover, in black-and-white, was the picture of the atomic bomb's mushroom cloud, with this title: *The Great Images of Our Time*. He began leafing through, somewhat reluctantly. First came an ad by two fashion designers showing a young man naked to the waist, which at first he thought was a great image of our time, but then there was the first true image of our time: the stone facade of a house in Hiroshima where because of the atomic bomb's heat the body of a man had liquefied, leaving his shadow imprinted there. He'd never seen this image and was astonished by it, feeling a kind of remorse: that thing had happened more than sixty years before, how was it possible he'd never seen it? The shadow on the stone was silhouetted, and in the profile he thought he could see his friend Ferruccio who on New Year's Eve of 1989, shortly before midnight, for no understandable reasons, had thrown himself from the tenth floor of a building onto via Cavour. Was it possible that the profile of Ferruccio, squashed into the soil on the thirty-first of December in nineteen ninety-nine, looked like the profile absorbed by stone in a Japanese city in nineteen forty-five? The idea was absurd, yet it passed through his mind in all its absurdity. He kept riffling the magazine, and meanwhile his heart began beating in a disorderly rhythm, one-two-pause, three-one-pause, two-three-one, pause-pause-two-three, the so-called extrasystole, nothing pathological, the cardiologist had reassured him after an entire day of testing, only a matter of anxiety. But now, why? It couldn't be those images provoking his emotions, they were faraway things. That naked girl with her arms raised who was running toward the camera in an apocalyptic landscape: he'd seen the image more than once without experiencing an impression so violent, yet now it produced in him an intense turmoil. He turned the page. At the edge of a pit was a man on his knees, palms together, a kid sadistically pointing a gun at his temple. Khmer Rouge, said the caption. To reassure himself he made himself think that these were things from faraway places and by now distant in time, but the thought wasn't enough, a strange form of emotion, which he almost thought was telling him the opposite, that the atrocity had happened yesterday, indeed it'd happened right that morning, while he was on this flight, and by sorcery had been imprinted on the page he was looking at. The voice of the loudspeaker stated that because of air traffic the landing would be delayed fifteen minutes, and meanwhile the passengers could enjoy the view. The plane traced a wide curve, banking to the right, from the little window opposite he could glimpse the blue of the sea while in his own, the white city of Athens was framed, with a green spot in the middle, no doubt a park, and then the Acropolis, he could see the Acropolis perfectly, and the Parthenon, his palms were damp, he asked himself if it weren't a sort of panic provoked by the plane going round in circles, and meanwhile he looked at the photo of a stadium where policemen in riot gear pointed submachine guns at a bunch of bare-footed men, under it was written: Santiago de Chile, 1973. And on the opposite page was a photo that seemed a montage, surely retouched, it couldn't be real, he'd never seen it: on the balcony of a nineteenth-century palazzo was Pope John Paul II next to a general in uniform. The Pope was without doubt the Pope, and the general was without doubt Pinochet, with that hair full of brilliantine, the chubby face, the little mustache, and the Ray-Ban sunglasses. The caption said: His Holiness the Pope on his official visit to Chile, April 1987. He began quickly leafing through the magazine, as though anxious to get to the end, almost without looking at the photographs, but he had to stop at one of them, it showed a kid with his back turned to a police van, his arms raised as though his beloved soccer team had scored a goal, but looking more closely one could see he was falling backwards, something stronger had struck him. On it was written: Genoa, July 2001, meeting of the eight richest countries in the world. The eight richest countries in the world: the phrase provoked in him a strange sensation, like something that is at once understandable and absurd, because it was understandable and yet absurd. Every photo was on a silvery page as though it were Christmas, with the date in big letters. He'd arrived at 2004, but he hesitated, he wasn't sure he wanted to see the next picture; was it possible that meanwhile the plane kept going around in circles? He turned the page, it showed a naked body collapsed on the ground, evidently a man though in the photo they'd blurred the pubic area, a soldier in camouflage extended a leg toward the body as though he were giving the boot to a garbage can, the dog he held on a leash was trying to bite a leg, the muscles of the animal were as taut as the cord that held it, in the other hand the soldier held a cigarette. The caption read: Abu Ghraib prison, Iraq, 2004. After that, he arrived at the year he found himself in now, the year of Our Lord 2008, that is he found himself in synch, that's what he thought even if he didn't know with what, but in synch. He couldn't tell what image he was in synch with, but he didn't turn the page, and meanwhile the plane was finally landing, he saw the strip running beneath him with the intermittent white bands blurring to a single band. He'd arrived.

Venizelos airport looked brand-new, surely they'd built it for the Olympic Games. He was happy with himself for being able to reach the boarding gate for Crete without reading the signs in English, the Greek he'd learned at school was still useful, curiously. When he landed at the Hania airport at first he didn't realize he'd reached his destination: during the brief flight from Athens to Crete, a little less than an hour, he'd fallen deeply asleep, forgetting everything, it seemed, even himself. To such a degree that when he came down the airplane's staircase into that African light, he asked himself where he was, and why he was there, and even who he was, and in that amazement at nothing he even felt happy. His suitcase wasn't long in arriving on the conveyor belt, just beyond the boarding gates were the car rental offices, he couldn't remember the instructions, Hertz or Avis? It was one or the other, fortunately he guessed right, along with the car keys they gave him a roadmap of Crete, a copy of the program of the convention, his hotel reservation, and the route to the tourist village where the convention-goers were lodged. Which by now he knew by heart, because he'd studied and restudied it in his guide, nicely furnished with roadmaps: from the airport you go down straight down to the coast, you have to go that way unless you want to go to the Marathi beaches, then you turn right, otherwise you end up west and he was going east, toward Iraklion, you pass in front of the Hotel Doma, go along Venizelos and follow the green signs that mean highway though it's actually a coastal freeway, you exit shortly after Georgopolis, a tourist spot to avoid, and follow the directions for the hotel, Beach Resort, it was easy.

The car, a black Volkswagen parked in the sun, was boiling, but he let it cool down a little by leaving the doors open, entered it as though he were late for an appointment, but he wasn't late and he hadn't any appointments, it was four o'clock in the afternoon, he'd get to the hotel in a little more than an hour, the convention wouldn't start til the evening of the following day, with an official banquet, he had more than twenty-four hours of freedom, what was the hurry? No hurry. After a few kilometers a tourist sign indicated the grave of Venizelos, a few hundred meters from the main road. He decided to take a short break to freshen up before the drive. Next to the entrance to the monument was an ice cream shop with a large open terrace overlooking the little town. He settled himself at a table, ordered a Turkish coffee and a lemon sorbet. The town he was looking at had been Venetian and then Turkish, it was nice, and of an almost blinding whiteness. Now he was feeling really good, with an unusual energy, the disquiet he'd felt on the plane had completely vanished. He checked the roadmap: to get to the freeway to Iraklion he could pass through the town or go around the gulf of Souda, a few kilometers more. He chose the second route, the gulf from up above was beautiful and the sea intensely azure. The descent from the hill to Souda was pleasant, beyond the low vegetation and the roofs of some houses he could see little coves of white sand, a strong urge to swim came over him, he turned off the air conditioning and lowered the window to feel on his face that warm air smelling of the sea. He passed the little industrial port and the residential zone and arrived at the intersection where, turning to the left, the road merged with the coastal highway to Iraklion. He put on his left blinker and stopped. A car behind him beeped for him to go: there was no oncoming traffic.

He didn't move forward, just let the car pass him, then signaled right and went in the opposite direction, where a sign said Mourniès.

And now we are following him, the unknown character who arrived in Crete to reach a pleasant seaside locale and who at a certain moment, abruptly, for a reason likewise unknown, took a road toward the mountains. The man proceeded till Mourniès, drove through the village without knowing where he was going though as if he did. Actually he wasn't thinking, just driving. He knew he was headed south: the sun, still high, was already behind him. Since he'd changed direction, that sensation of lightness had returned which, for a few moments, he'd felt at the table in the ice cream shop, looking down on the broad horizon: an unusual lightness, and with it an energy of which he kept no memory, as though he'd returned to being young again, a sort of light euphoria, almost a small happiness. He arrived at a village called Fournès, drove through the town confidently as though he already knew the road, stopped at a crossroads, the main road went to the right, he took the secondary road whose sign said: Lefka Ori, the white mountains. He went on calmly, the sensation of well-being was turning into a sort of cheerfulness, a Mozart aria came to mind and he felt he could reproduce its notes, he began whistling them with a facility that amazed him, but then went hopelessly out of tune in a couple of passages, which made him laugh. The road slipped into the rugged canyons of a mountain. They were beautiful and wild places, the car went along a narrow asphalt road bordering the bed of a dry creek, at a certain point the creek-bed disappeared amidst the rocks and the asphalt ended in a dirt road, in a barren plain amidst inhospitable mountains, meanwhile the light was fading, but he kept going as though he already knew the way, like someone obeying an old memory or an order received in a dream, and at a certain point on a crooked pole he saw a sign riddled with holes as if by gunshots or by time, and the sign said: Monastiri.

He followed it as though it were what he awaited til he saw a tiny monastery, its roof in ruins. He realized he'd arrived. Went down. The dilapidated door of those ruins hung inward. He figured by now in that place there was no one any longer, a beehive under the little portico seemed the only housekeeper. He went down and waited as though he had an appointment. It was almost dark. Then at the door a monk appeared, he was very old and moved with difficulty, he had the look of an anchorite, with hair to his shoulders and a yellowish beard, what do you want, he asked in Greek. Do you know Italian?, answered the traveler. The old man nodded. A little, he murmured. I've come to change places with you, said the man.

So it'd been like this, and no other conclusion was possible, because that story didn't call for any other possible conclusions, but the person who knew this story was aware that he couldn't let it conclude in this way, and at this point he made a leap in time. And thanks to one of those leaps in time that are possible only in the imagination, things landed in the future with regard to that month of April of 2008. How many years ahead no one knows, and the person who knew the story remained vague, twenty years, for instance, which in the lifetime of a man is a lot because if in 2008 a man of sixty still has all his energy, in 2028 he'll be an old man, his body worn out by time.

And so the person who knew this story imagined the story's continuation, and so let's accept that we're in 2028, as the person who knew the story had wanted and had imagined it would continue.

And at this point, the person who imagined the continuation of this story saw two young people, a guy and a girl wearing leather shorts and trekking boots, who were hiking in the mountains of Crete. The girl said to her companion: I think that old guide you found in your father's library doesn't make any sense, by now the monastery will be a pile of stones full of lizards, why don't we head toward the sea? And the guy responded: I think you're right. But just as he said this she replied: no, let's keep on for a bit, you never know. And in fact it was enough to walk around the rugged hill of red stones that cut through the countryside and there it was, the monastery, or rather its ruins, and the two of them advanced, within the canyons blew a wind that raised dust, the monastery's door had collapsed, wasps' nests defended that empty cave, the two of them had already turned their backs on that gloom when they heard a voice. In the empty space of the door stood a man. He was very old, looked dreadful, with a long white beard to his chest and hair down to his shoulders. Oooh, called the voice. Nothing else. The couple stood still. The man asked: do you understand Italian? They didn't respond. What happened in 2008?, asked the old man. The two young people looked at each other, they didn't have the courage to exchange a word. Do you have photographs?, asked the old man, what happened in 2008? Then he gestured as if to send them away, though perhaps he was brushing away the wasps that whirled under the portico, and he returned to the dark of his cave.

The man who knew this story was aware that it couldn't finish in any other way. Before writing his stories, he loved telling them to himself. And he'd tell them to himself so perfectly, with all the details, word by word, that one could say they were written in his memory. He'd tell them to himself preferably late in the evening, in the solitude of that big empty house, or on certain nights when he couldn't reach sleep, those nights in which insomnia conceded nothing but imagination, not much, yet imagination gave him a reality so alive that it seemed more real than the reality he was living. But the most difficult thing wasn't telling himself his stories, that was easy, it was as though he'd see the words of the stories he told himself written on the dark screen of his room, when fantasy would keep his eyes open. And that one story, which he'd told himself in this way so many times, seemed to him an already printed book, one that was easy to express mentally but very hard to write with the letters of the alphabet required for the thought to be made concrete and visible. It was as if he were lacking the principle of reality to write his story, and in order to live the effective reality of what was real within him yet unable to become truly real, he'd chosen this place.

His trip was planned in fine detail. He landed at the Hania airport, got his luggage, went into the Hertz office, picked up the car keys. Three days?, the clerk asked, astonished. What's so strange, he said. No one comes to Crete on vacation for three days, the clerk replied smiling. I have a long weekend, he responded, for what I have to do it's enough.

It was beautiful, the light in Crete. It wasn't Mediterranean but African; he'd reach the Beach Resort in an hour and a half, at most two, even going slowly he'd arrive there around six, a shower and he'd start writing immediately, the hotel restaurant was open til eleven, it was Thursday evening, he counted: all of Friday, Saturday, and Sunday, three full days. They'd be enough: in his head everything was already written.

Why he turned left at that light he coudn't have explained. The pylons of the freeway were clearly visible, another four or five hundred meters and he'd be at the coastal freeway to Iraklion. But instead he turned left, where a little blue sign indicated an unknown place. He thought he'd already been there, for in a moment he saw everything: a tree-lined street with a few houses, a plain square with an ugly monument, a ledge of rocks, a mountain. It was a flash of lightning. That strange thing which medical science can't explain, he told himself, they call it *déjà vu*, an already-seen, it'd never happened to me before. But the explanation he gave himself didn't reassure him, because the already-seen endured, it was stronger than what he was seeing, like a membrane wrapping the surrounding reality, the trees, the mountains, the evening shadows, even the air he was breathing. He felt overcome by vertigo and was afraid of being sucked into it, but only for a moment, because as it expanded, that sensation went through a strange metamorphosis, like a glove turning inside out and bringing forth the hand it was covering. Everything changed perspective, in a flash he felt the euphoria of discovery, a subtle nausea, and a mortal melancholy. But also a sense of infinite liberation, as when we finally understand something we'd known all along and didn't want to know: it wasn't the already-seen that was swallowing him in a never-lived past, it was he who was capturing it in a future yet to be lived. As he drove among the olive trees on that little road that was taking him toward the mountains, he knew that at a certain point he'd find an old rusty sign full of holes on which was written: Monastiri. And that he'd follow it. Now everything was clear.

Henning Ahrens, an experienced novelist, poet, and translator in Peine, Germany, is the author of six books. The winner of numerous prizes, his poems are full of "Sprachfreude, Sinnlichkeit und Ironie" (the joy of language, sensuality, and irony).

Briefe an den Wirt

1

Briefe an den Wirt geschrieben.
Unumwunden zugegeben,
daß mich Hunger quälte, Hunger

auf den Umlaut: auf Vokale
wie Opale und Türkise,
wie Rubine. Bärenhunger

auf das Glitzern fetter Klunker,
aufs Gefunkel von Geschmeide,
dunkle Pracht und Üppigkeiten,

sättigend wie schwere Speisen.
Stift in leere Suppenschüsseln
eingetunkt und losgekritzelt

—Briefe an den Wirt.

Letters to the Host

1

Letters written to the host.
Unequivocal confession:
hunger tormented me, hunger

for the umlaut: for vowels
like opals and turquoises,
like rubies. Hungry as a bear

for the twinkle of fat trinkets,
for the brilliance of baubles,
dark magnificence and opulence,

satisfying as a scrumptious meal.
Pencil plunged into empty
tureens, scribbling, scribbling

—Letters to the host.

2

Jedes fremde Wort vermieden
in den Briefen. War nicht schwierig,

denn ich kannte nicht sehr viele.
Alle Wörter, die ich kannte,

wuchsen irgendwo auf Feldern,
wucherten wie Melde, schossen

plötzlich auf in Wiesen,
knospig, schotig. Abgedroschen

waren alle, leere Hülsen,
ausgeworfen nach den Schüssen

auf die Dinge. Trotzdem schrieb ich,
denn sie trieben dunkle Blüten

unter meinen Händen, Ähren,
voll mit schwarzen Körnern,

und ich füllte meine Taschen,
bis sie aus den Nähten platzten.

Briefe an den Wirt geschrieben:
Seitenweise Kraut und Rüben.

2

Every outlandish word avoided
in the letters. Not too hard

because I didn't know very many.
All the words I did know

sprouted somewhere in fields,
sprang up like spinach, shot up

suddenly in meadows,
budded, podded. All were

hulled, empty shells,
discarded after my best

shot at the lot. Yet I wrote
because they pressed dark blossoms

under my hands, and ears
full of black kernels,

and I filled my pockets
till they burst at the seams.

Letters written to the host:
notebook leaves strewn with word roots and stems.

3

Horizonttendenz unendlich,
dennoch Grenzen ohne Ende:
Haustür, Hoftor, Weidezäune,

ein Klavier, das niemand spielte,
Geige mit kaputten Saiten,
Bücher, wie sie Menschen lesen,

die nicht lesen, Ölgemälde
—Schwan auf rotem Blättermeer,
Reiterschar auf Nebelweg.

Horizonttendenz unendlich,
dennoch Grenzen ohne Ende
in der Landschaftsleere: Wege,

wie die Läufe von Gewehren,
trennten Äcker von den Wäldern,
Halmspalier von Baumkohorte.

Trotzdem an den Wirt geschrieben,
auf den Knien im Dreck gelegen,
losgeheult und angefleht.

(Hat sich keiner drum geschert.)

3

Horizon stretched unending,
but boundaries without end:
front door, front gate, pasture fences,

a piano no one played,
violin with broken strings,
books read by people

who don't read, oil paintings
—swan on red paper sea,
host of riders on the great cloud way.

Horizon stretched unending,
but boundaries without end
in the empty landscape: pathways

like gun barrels
divided farmlands from forests,
trellised plant from stand of trees.

Nonetheless written to the host,
down on my knees in muck,
having howled and begged.

(And no one cared for it.)

4

Briefe an den Wirt geschrieben
und im Wald herumgetrieben,
sieben an der Zahl, ich weiß noch:

Setzling neben Setzling, Pfähle
hielten Maschendrähte,
um den Wildfraß einzudämmen,

Blätter lagen zwischen Stämmen,
satzverstümmelt, unbeendet.
(Unterschrieben waren alle.)

Shreie gellten, Sägen kreischten,
Waldarbeiter schlugen Schneisen,
sieben an der Zahl, ich weiß noch:

Auf der Lichtung, himmelüber,
Rotwild, Fuchs and Eichelhäher,
Pfotenspuren auf den Blättern,

halb vermodert, dünne Adern,
von den Sägen durchgeschnitten
—Briefe an den Wirt.

4

Letters written to the host
and after swinging through the woods
I still know seven things:

seedling beside seedling, netting
strung on posts to check
the damage done by deer,

leaves lying between trunks,
mutilated sentence fragments.
(All were signed.)

Shouts echoed, saws squealed,
foresters hacked firebreaks,
I still know seven things:

at the clearing, sky above,
red deer, fox, and jay,
paw prints on the leaves,

half-rotted, thin-ribbed,
saw-severed
—letters to the host.

5

Tief im Stall. Der Kalk der Silben
reiselte und Wände schwitzten
Wörter aus, die ungelesen
in die Schwemmentmistung trieften.

Bullen rammten ihre Hörner
in den Trost der Nachbarkörper.

Nester an den Eisensäulen.
Schwalben schossen durch die Gänge,
Bandwurmsätze in den Schnäbeln,
Punkte, dick wie Stubenfliegen.

Bullen tauchten ihre Schnauzen
in den Trost der Futtertröge.

Futterkiste, voll mit Briefen,
stand vorm Fenster. Bullen fraßen,
bis sie endlich schlachtreif waren
und den Bolzenschuß bekamen.

Und die Schädel sackten tiefer
in den Trost zerkauter Wörter.

Briefe an den Wirt geschrieben,
zwischen Schwalbenruf und Brüllen,
in der Kammer, wo die Kannen
leer vor grauen Mauern standen.

5

Way back in the barn. The whitewash of syllables
trickled gently and the walls sweated
words which dripped unread
into the watery ooze.

Bulls rammed their horns
into the comfort of their neighbors.

Nests on the iron support columns.
Swallows shot through the openings,
run-on sentences in their beaks,
periods thick as houseflies.

Bulls dipped their muzzles
into the comfort of their mangers.

Feed crates full of letters
stood before the window. Bulls ate
till they were finally ripe for slaughter
and received the stungun's bolt.

And their skulls settled deeper
into the comfort of chewed-up words.

Letters written to the host
between swallow call and cattle bellow
in the pantry where the jugs
stood empty by the gray walls.

6

Heimlich sind wir ausgestiegen
aus dem Haus, durch Nebelwände.
Bücher in der Hand,
Verträge,

die uns Äcker überschrieben,
Wohnhaus, Scheunen, Ställe, Garten,
Wasserwiesen, Waldanteile.

Alles in den Wind geschossen
und die Pforte aufgeschlossen,
rechts vom Tor,
hindurchgeschlichen,

Taschen voller Spreu, im Schädel
nichts als Wirbelwinde,

um dem Wirt zu schreiben: Briefe
voller Halbwahrheiten,
voller Ignorantenträume.

Irgendwie zu spät gekommen
und den falschen Zug genommen,
der uns nicht ans Ziel der Briefe
brachte, sondern Runden drehte,

rund ums Haus,
das, frisch verklinkert,
einem neuen Wirt gehörte.

6

Secretly we have gotten out,
out of the house through walls of mist.
Books in hand,
deeds

ceding us the farmlands,
house, sheds, barns, garden,
water meadows, wood plots.

All gone with the wind
and us slinking through
the unlocked door
to the right of the gate,

pockets full of chaff, nothing
in the skull but whirlwinds

for writing to the host: letters
full of half truths,
full of ignorant dreams.

Somehow come too late
and on the wrong train
which brought us not to the letters' goal
but circled round and round the house

which, freshly re-sided,
belonged to a new landlord,
a different host.

7

Briefe an den Wirt geschrieben,
blind vor Licht.

Im Schatten, hinten,
sah ich tintige Gestalten,

hörte ich ein Flügelschlagen
—wer war Gast und wer war Wirt?

Schlag der Flügel
auf den Nacken,

Federn, naß wie Scheuerlappen.
Plötzlich brüllte eine Stimme:

Ich bin Gast,
und du bist Wirt!

Briefe and den Wirt geschrieben,
unumwunden zugegeben,
losgeheult und angefleht.
Doch ich hatte mich geirrt.

7

Letters written to the host,
blind before the light.

Behind, in the shadow,
I saw inky forms,

I heard a beating of wings
—who was guest and who was host?

The wing beat
on the nape of my neck,

feathers wet as scrubcloths.
Suddenly a voice bellowed:

I am guest,
and you are host!

Letters written to the host,
unequivocal confession,
having howled and begged.
But I was wrong.

Marcos Giralt Torrente was born in Madrid in 1968. In his novels, stories, and forth-coming memoir Father and Son: A Lifetime, *he writes with deliberation and intensity about love and family.* McSweeney's *published his story collection* The End of Love *in 2013.*

Tiempo de vida

Lo peor no avisa pero tampoco engaña. Cuando se presenta, intenta-mos no verlo, pero en el fondo sabemos que ha llegado, que está ahí, y que todo lo que hagamos para zafarnos solamente servirá para ter-minar aceptándolo (la constante invocación de algo, aunque sea para negarlo, nos habitúa a ello, de forma que cuando se hace irrevocable es ya la única realidad que vivimos). Nosotros no fuimos distintos. Cuando lo peor le llegó, ninguno de quienes estábamos al lado de mi padre quisimos verlo. Amigos, conocidos, todo el mundo nos ayudaba. Ne sé quién había tenido lo mismo, o conocía a alguien que lo había tenido, y lo había superado. Incluso los médicos consentían que fan-taseásemos con la excepción, con el mejor pronóstico. Es una realidad paralela: la negación sabiendo. Uno escucha lo que los médicos dicen, memoriza todas las posibilidades y finalmente acaba quedándose con la más favorable. Uno escucha frases forzadas como que *no hay estadísticas*, como que *siempre cabe la sorpresa*, y en consecuencia es imposible no especular, incluso, con la curación total. Aunque sepas que no, aunque la mirada con la que fueron dichas prácticamente la excluyera. Cabe la sorpresa, sí, nos quieren decir, pero mejor no esperarla. Y, como no quieres creer, acudes a otras consultas, buscas otros pareceres, movilizas a todo el que tiene un amigo médico . . .

Father and Son: A Lifetime

The worst comes without warning but also without deception. When it comes, we try not to see it, but deep down we know that it's come, it's here, and in the end everything we do to try to escape it just prepares us to accept it (the constant invoking of something, if only to reject it, accustoms us to it, so that by the time it becomes irrevocable it's the only reality we know). We were no different. When the worst came, none of us who were close to my father wanted to acknowledge it. Friends, acquaintances, everyone abetted us. Somebody had been given the same diagnosis, or knew someone who had been, who had recovered. Even the doctors allowed us to fantasize about the exception, the best possible outcome. It's a parallel reality: willful denial. You hear what the doctors say, you memorize all the possibilities, and what you're left with in the end is the most desirable one. You hear hollow statements like *there are no statistics*, or *there's always room for surprise*, on the basis of which it's impossible not to speculate; about a complete recovery, even. Though you know better; though the look with which these things are said essentially rules it out. There's room for surprise, yes, the look says, but it's best not to expect it. And since you don't want to take their word for it, you consult other doctors, seek out second opinions, recruit anyone who has a doctor friend who might be able to help you, and at the end of the road you're back where you started with a few less days left to live intensely.

2005 is the fateful year.

In 2004 I'm living three hundred miles from Madrid, in a town in the province of Valencia where, after sitting for her examinations, my wife has gotten a job as a philosophy teacher. Though both of us try to look on the bright side, it isn't easy: we face several years in limbo until she can enter a transfer lottery. My wife feels guilty and I'm not always able to hide my frustration.

In 2004 I get angry with my father for the last time, about the painting that he offered to sell after visiting me in Berlin. I find a buyer and he keeps his word and gives me half the money, but it bothers me that he needs to justify it to the friend he met in Brazil by telling her that it's the wedding present he didn't give me when I got married a year ago.

Between 2004 and 2005 I make many calls to the contractor, the architect, and the town hall to finalize the preparations for the rebuilding of the house that my mother and I have bought in Galicia as a place for her to live when she retires.

Between 2004 and 2005 I have the feeling that I'm facing upheavals that will change my life and I'm not always optimistic about them. It unsettles me to have left Madrid when my mother is preparing to move away; it unsettles me not to know how long my wife and I will have to live in furnished rental apartments; it unsettles me that my bond with my mother, crucial up until now, will become less tight; and it unsettles me that the huge effort that I put into my books, the outflow of time and mental energy, shouldn't be properly rewarded. For the first time everything seems about to fall into place (my mother's fate is almost resolved, my wife's and mine is taking shape), but I feel tired and I'm afraid I won't have the reserves for the fast-approaching future.

In February my new novel comes out and over the next few

months I travel frequently to Madrid from my Valencian exile. I make myself available for the few publicity activities; I visit my mother's younger brother, who has cancer; I go out at night; and I travel to Galicia to deal with the contractor.

In April my uncle dies and my father attends the burial with my mother and me. He's affected by my uncle's death, but I also notice his impatience. He isn't at ease, he can't remove himself from the picture, he views any misfortune as a threat.

In May we don't see each other and at the beginning of June he calls to say that he's already left the city for the summer and he invites my wife and me to visit. The ritual of past years is repeated. I don't turn him down flat, but both of us know that I won't go. It bothers me that he hasn't let me know in time to give us the chance to meet in Madrid. My summer, shorter than his, is spent in Galicia, in the town where we'll at last begin work on my mother's house in September.

Upon our return everything begins to happen quickly. My wife is back at her school on September 1 and I follow her a month later. Various matters—and a bit of foot-dragging—keep me in Madrid. The novel hasn't done as well as expected, and after the quiet of summer, my hopes give way to discouragement. Except for work assignments, which I complete with more haste than diligence, over the course of the month all I do is flail about, losing myself in the chaos of anxiety, the labyrinth of possibilities. I go out too much at night and I'm in no mood to shut myself up with another book, something that I inevitably associate with the place where my wife is waiting for me. My wake-up call comes in the form of a stumble at six in the morning in a bar that passes for underground; whether it is or not, what it most resembles is a black hole that you reach already defeated by the responsibilities of the approaching day and from which you emerge hours later with the certainty that once again you've behaved like an idiot. That night I sit down on a sofa near the door to talk to a Russian who says something to me, and as I'm getting up to join the friends

I'm with, I trip and split open my chin. To judge by the scar, the cut probably needed stitches. But all I do is cover it with a napkin, and when I leave the place an hour later, I head not to a clinic but home.

I say that this is my wake-up call because from now on I get hold of myself, and though I'm still in low spirits, I begin preparations for my departure. Among other things, I say good-bye to my father and invite him again to come and visit us. He doesn't reject the offer, but he's so vague about when he might be able to come, without offering any convincing reason, that it's as if he had. Still, we're in a good place. Not just any good place but one that I expect to be permanent, ever since three years ago in Berlin I made the decision to wall off the problem between us from our interactions. Tired of mistrust, I've decided to try giving up my eternal touchiness, which I believe is justified but which dooms us to a difficult relationship, subject to shifts in mood, silences, and mutual trepidation. It's taken me three years to prove to him that our lunches are no longer minefields; with some incredulity he's gotten used to the fact that my hitherto rare visits to his house have become rather more frequent; and just this fall, when he has two years left to live but we don't know it yet, I have the feeling that he's finally let down his guard. Since his return to Madrid I've visited him twice and I've even gone so far as to inform him of my unsettled state. I tell him about staying out too late, and he responds, surprised that I'm confiding in him but scrupulously playing the role that he believes I want him to play. He invokes his own example and assures me that he regrets the time he's wasted in his life. He tells me that he hasn't worked as much as he should have and that the things we pursue in periods of confusion are worthless: vain distractions that sooner or later fade. He tells me that I have talent, a promising career, a wife who supports me, and that it's absurd to lose any more time. All of this he says in a low voice, not so much to prevent the friend he met in Brazil from hearing us as to stress the importance of what he's saying and leave no room for doubt. It's a curious situation, something completely new. My father—whom I've never allowed into my private life, as punishment for all the times he failed me—is giving me advice and for the first time unabashedly donning the mantle of father. Even better, leery of the authority that I've granted him, he's acting more like an occasional confidant than a father. It's the only way. I'm thirty-seven and he's sixty-five, and though his presence in my life may have been constant, it's been so at a comfortable distance, on a very secondary level: he hasn't shared the tribulations my mother has had to endure on my account; he hasn't known the daily uncertainty that children bring; he hasn't seen me suffer or cry; he's had little to do with my hopes or my joys; he doesn't know my friends; he doesn't know me.

It's on my last visit that September—once my late-night drifting has come to an end and neither his advice nor my expressions of regret are necessary any longer, since I've decided to leave, break away, go back to my wife in search of a new routine—when he informs me of the first sign of his illness. He does it so unobtrusively that I hardly notice. I've said that it wasn't like him to clamor for the spotlight, to voice his worries. If this time he does, I can't rule out the possibility that it's his contribution to the new climate of trust, that he's repaying my revelations of the last few days with an equivalent disclosure. Whatever the case, the matter barely occupies the time it takes to be expressed and it isn't until after I've left Madrid, in our phone conversations at the beginning of October, that it acquires substance in the face of his growing apprehension. His general practitioner has ordered a test, but he has to wait too long for it, the symptoms aren't letting up, and since in the meantime his alarm has grown, he decides to consult a private doctor. By then my involvement is complete. I encourage him to go as soon as possible and on the day of the appointment, when we talk on the phone, he tells me with ill-disguised distress that they've found a cyst and that, though they've assured him that it's not necessarily malignant, an operation has to be scheduled immediately. I try to calm him with impromptu arguments, but he doesn't listen. He tells me that when it was time to pay the bill, the doctor refused to take any money, claiming that it was because he had no private insurance. That settles it. Each of us is seized by the same dark foreboding; each of us senses it in the other just as so many times over the course of our lives each has felt what the other felt or thought without having to say a word. We are completely connected, as always, but for the first time we fear the same thing, hope for the same thing.

Then comes the anxiety, the frenzy of getting the operation to happen quickly, locating the best surgeon, trying to find evidence in the experiences of others to counter our premonitions of doom.

My father is nervous. The friend he met in Brazil is nervous. I'm nervous. Though we don't say so to one another, we know that the worst is here. We're like performers, overplaying our roles. My father, the friend he met in Brazil, and me. My father lets down his final defenses and for the first time accepts my help without reservations, even demands it. He's grateful, vulnerable. The friend he met in Brazil gets an inkling that I might be useful in the days to come and for the first time she invites me to visit whenever I like. With an attempt at a girlish smile she tells me that the only thing that makes my father forget the wait is my company. I'm presented with the opportunity to prove that my readiness for sacrifice is as great as my past demands and for the first time I don't hold back. I don't stop to consider the consequences presented by the future into which we're advancing. I think, of course, and on occasion my thoughts are egotistical, but immediately I rebel and make an effort to cancel out any petty calculation with my actions. I suppose that I've speculated so often about this moment that I proceed like someone who's been programmed, like a zombie obeying the commands of his master. I call him every day and, if I'm in Madrid, I visit him in the evenings; I try to entertain him.

The time for the operation arrives and my father prepares for it with his usual resignation. Earlier, he'd begun gradually to involve me in the doctor appointments leading up to the operation. For some reason, he trusts me more than the friend he met in Brazil. It must be that I retain more information, I explain the things that he hasn't understood, I look for solutions, I answer his questions promptly, I'm ready with the most innocuous interpretation. I'm not a caretaker who requires care myself, and he puts his trust in me, responds in kind. The night before the operation, at the hospital, he gives me his bag to keep, invites me to withdraw money from his account if necessary, explains his financial situation, and puts up only a token resistance when I offer to sleep there. Later that same night, as I try to fall asleep in a chair next to his bed, I want to make some pledge in exchange for everything coming out all right, but I can't. I'm afraid to make a promise that I know I won't keep. It's strange. I'm someone who spends his life thinking, trying to keep one step ahead, and I can't allow myself to speculate. Out of fear, but also because I'm still setting my priorities against his. It's my final moment of resistance. A testament to times past.

From now on, without realizing it, I become his father. In the morning I help him to shower. He's in good spirits, he wants to do everything right, and my help reinforces his determination. It brings us closer to success. If all is right between us, everything else will be right too. The friend he met in Brazil appears shortly before they come to get him and I note his impatience with the intrusion of a reality separate from the hospital routine that we've become a part of after our night of initiation.

I think this is the key to everything that happens next. I don't linger on the periphery; I accompany him to the very center of his suffering.

I am his father and he is my son. No one knows what the future holds, but it seems that as long as he's weak and sick he'll seek my protection. Is he following my lead or am I following his? Is he setting the pace or am I paving the way for his surrender with my own?

He holds my hand until he enters the operating room and I can't help taking comfort in his deference. While he's inside my aunt comes, my wife comes, a friend of hers comes, my mother doesn't come so as not to upset the friend my father met in Brazil, but she waits at home for news from us. All the promises that I didn't make the night before I make now, walking the hallways, counting the tiles, stepping on only some of them according to a predetermined order.

When the surgeon emerges, I'm the first to spot him. He leads the friend my father met in Brazil and me into his office, and there's no need for him to speak the words he's already speaking. The friend my father met in Brazil is sobbing and I try to contain myself but in the end I'm overcome when I ask the practical questions, the questions about time that make doctors most uncomfortable. I feel wrenched apart, outside myself. The person speaking, acting, isn't me. I don't know what goes through my mind. Everything and nothing. When I leave the office, I hug the friend my father met in Brazil and we promise to forget our differences, to pull together from now on. She asks me to keep on top of her, to constantly be telling her what she should do, and in the first place we agree not to tell my father how little time the doctor says he has left. It's clear that this is all too much for her. *What will become of me?* she asks insistently. She can't hide what for now is her main concern: loneliness.

The worst moment comes that afternoon in the ICU. We enter wearing surgical masks and my father smiles, flashing a V for victory. He doesn't seem to consider that the news might be anything other than good. But before the end of the time we've been allotted, he asks the friend he met in Brazil to leave us alone. I don't know why. He doesn't say anything to me, doesn't ask me anything. I try to act cheerful, like him, but I'm not sure whether I succeed. I start training myself to dole out information in bits. I explain that they've removed the tumor, but there are still some nodes that will have to be treated with chemotherapy.

It's what he would want. Or so I believe. His ancestral refusal to verbalize drama allows me to think so. He couldn't handle it.

Over the next few days I continue the tightrope walk of preparing him for what's to come without dashing the hopes that his wide-open eyes plead for, alert to any sign from me. I spend most of my time with him. We've made a schedule to take turns by his side and the friend he met in Brazil is supposed to be with him in the mornings, but it's Christmas, a sister who lives abroad has come to stay, and she begins to cut short her visits. There are even days when she doesn't come. On Christmas Eve she doesn't, and my mother and I have dinner at the hospital.

It's too early to accuse her of desertion and I play it down when my father expresses his surprise, but I can't help some rejoicing when my lack of faith in her is confirmed yet again. She also mounts strange maneuvers that I notice and that my father must notice too. One morning when we run into each other at the hospital she invites me to breakfast and tells me that when my father is gone she'll help me in any way she can. It's clear that gears are turning in her head and she's already contemplating a future without him. She vacillates, caught between two impulses: on the one hand, the need to create a strategy that will require her to become more involved than she is, and on the other, her inability to act selflessly. Probably she's begun to talk to lawyers, or her family is giving her advice, and she gets confused trying to listen to everyone. One minute she's fleeing, gone, and the next she demands unrealistic degrees of responsibility.

One day all of a sudden my father asks me for his bag, which I still have in my keeping. One day all of a sudden his dread reappears. One afternoon he's in a state of terror when I come in. He's read a report that the friend he met in Brazil shouldn't have given him, and though the medical jargon prevents him from understanding the full gravity of his case, he's managed to grasp that more organs are affected than we'd let on. I place great stress on the word "microscopic," which appears in the report, and he calms down, but in his eyes there's a shadow of suspicion, defeat, and desolation that will never go away. On another visit he tells me that the friend he met in Brazil has informed him that he's very sick and he's going to die. As he hopes, I flatly deny that this is true. The following days, he asks me again and sets traps that I don't fall into. Each time it's harder to keep my footing. So hard do I work to protect him that there are moments when even I begin to believe that there's hope. I think about miracles. I think that if time is on our side a full recovery might still be possible. But it doesn't last. Often, when I'm alone, I cry. In the Metro all I have to do is walk past a street musician to fall apart. I feel remote from everything, especially other people. I can't forget that not long from now the day will come when my father won't be here. I feel his defenselessness as my own and it makes me even sadder to think that his life has been incomplete, that he'll exit it unfulfilled, with business left undone. I know this is a presumption that I'll never be able to confirm, but that's what makes me saddest. Not so much the loss of him as the possibility that he'll die with the feeling that he's been a failure.

Anne Parian is a writer, photographer, and videographer currently living in Paris, France. The author of twelve books, Parian uses the medium of poetry to explore different artistic states, interweaving fiction, nonfiction, and photography.

Monospace

Que l'on me demande ce que c'est
n'étant pas jardinière pas architecte ni historienne je réponds
    exceptionnellement

Temps d'éclosions et suites d'arrosages pour en décrire les étapes
    ma curiosité ou l'ennui dans mes choix ne changent rien

ce que je souhaite non plus

J'adopte une mixité des temps que les acteurs habiles à se distraire
    ou à l'avoir été agissent sans confusion d'effets
levés pour courir
attardés sur des bancs

observez l'action de l'un sur celle supposée de l'autre

un programme constructiviste clair
aussitôt vieilli regretté pourquoi en un temps continu dont
    j'apprécie mal le terme

Monospace

They ask me what it is
my answer is odd because I'm not a gardener or an architect or an
    historian

Hatchings in season and sprinklers in rows describe the stages
    where my worry and curiosity change nothing

I'm no longer hoping

I go for a blend of states that those now or once good at
    entertaining enact without any confusion of effects
rising to run
resting on benches

observe one's actions on the supposed other

a clear constructivist system
soon outdated I regretted why in real time can't I see the end

Je reprends

et calque traditionnelles mes réalisations sur les styles historiques
familiers véritablement altérés de réminiscences anecdotiques
avec la conviction de réussir quelque chose sérieusement

Je transporte tout le petit matériel

de nombreux objets que je sais associer en de nombreux exemples
dans l'hypothèse d'une suite

quant à des fins de liberté

I begin again

and trace my creations in the dramatically altered familiar historical
styles of anecdotal memory sure of seriously succeeding

I move all the small stuff

the many objects I know how to put together in many ways in the
synthesis of a hypothesis

concerning the limits of liberty

Vous iriez divaguant
à travers les imitations trucages simulacres rejoindre une dimension
  écartée de la perspective

feignant d'objectiver le point de fuite
filant visuellement en deux dimensions

éclairs et fortunes
insolites dans leurs conditions empiriques

j'écarte
ou associe éléments
et principes
sans hésitation quant à la férocité prêtée aux figures qui me
  ressemblent

Je dispose des moyens de mes réalisations comme idéales décris le
  paysage minuscule avec l'intention de le saturer de tout

badigeon

Je suis le peintre

You go rambling
through imitations confabulations simulacra to reach a dimension
    far from perspective

making the vanishing point into an object
filing off in two directions

flashes and fortunes
unusual in their useful state

I spread out
and associate elements
and principles
not worrying about the ferocious figures that look like me

My creations are my ideals I describe the minute countryside
    saturating it with everything

whitewash

I am its painter

Je n'en suis pas le peintre

badigeon

du plus proche
comme apparu lointain
chercher des raccourcis

Je marche dans la dimension plate quelque chose de souple sous les
    pieds et quelques lignes élastiques croisées sous les pas

élémentaires

Je dispose volumes et décors arbitrairement et peux rester sans
    réponse sur la raison d'une chose ou l'autre

I am not its painter

whitewash

up close
looks farther
look for shortcuts

I walk in a flat dimension something soft under foot and pliant
lines intersecting beneath my steps

elementary

I arrange spaces and scenery arbitrarily giving no reason for my
choices

Dubbed "the most outstanding young author in Hong Kong," Hon Lai Chu writes award-winning Kafkaesque tales of life in a hypermodern dystopia. Written with precision and economy, these surrealistic stories' sense of malaise is both specific and universal.

林木椅子

「這世上再也沒有甚麼，會比林木的肚腹更柔軟，更容易令人對睡眠著魔。」I遺憾地對林木的母親林園說。那個因年邁而事事沉著面對的母親剛剛告訴I，林木已正式成為了一張椅子，隨著一批大量生產的高級家具，傾銷到海外國家。

「還有甚麼事呢？」老母親開始不耐煩。I喃喃地說：「我想買下他……」但老母親已經關上了門。

I不會忘記，那個雨絲向橫傾瀉的午後，他初次把僵硬的頸椎和纏滿死結的頭顱緊緊地靠著林木屈曲而成了小山丘似的雙腿。I感到自己的身子逐漸輕軟而小，像一縷煙那樣上升、懸浮，成了無處不在的微粒。

而林木躺在地上，腹部承托著I，蒼白的天空就在上方，烏雲迅速地移動，他想起了一些從未發生的事和不曾見過的人面，時間總是如此過去。直至坐在他身上的人突然站起來，舒展發麻的手腳。林木張開眼睛，才知道綿密的水串已滿布窗外的世界，四周結聚了牛奶混合泥土的味道。

「疲倦感好像已停止擴散。」I的手按著頸項，把頭顱甩了幾下後說。林木站在辦公桌的後方，他對職業性而不帶多餘感情聲音的掌握已經熟能生巧：「疲倦感正慢慢地集結，但是要完全清除還要花上好一段時間。下星期再來吧。」…

Forrest Woods, Chair

"There's nothing in this world that's softer than Forrest Woods's belly, nothing that leaves you more susceptible to the charms of sleep," *I* said wistfully to Woods's mother, Mrs. Woods. The mother, left imperturbable by her advanced age, had just informed *I* that Forrest Woods had officially become a chair, and was being dumped on the foreign market, along with a large quantity of mass-produced, high quality furniture.

"Is there anything else?" Mrs. Woods was getting impatient. *I* mumbled, "I wanted to buy him..." But the old woman had already shut the door.

I would never forget the wet and blustery afternoon when, for the first time, he had rested his stiff neck and tensely knotted head against Forrest Woods's legs, which the latter had bent to resemble little hillocks. *I* had felt his body gradually get lighter and smaller, rising and floating like a wisp of smoke, turning into tiny particles that went everywhere.

Woods lay on the ground, with his body supporting *I*, and above him the washed out sky, where dark clouds moved swiftly, and he thought of things that had never happened and faces he'd never seen, and the time always passed in this way. Until the moment arrived when the person sitting on him abruptly stood up and stretched his or her arms and legs, which had fallen asleep. Woods opened his eyes to find that dense ropes of rain now blanketed the world outside the window, and the air all around was clotted with the scent of mud mixed with milk.

"The fatigue seems to have stopped spreading," *I* said after pressing on his neck and twisting his head around a few times. Woods was standing behind a desk. Through practice, he had mastered a tone of voice that was both professional and not overly emotional. He said: "The fatigue is slowly resolving, but it will take some time to clear up completely. Come back next week."

The man then staggered out of Woods's office.

Long before *I* rang the door bell, Forrest Woods had looked out the window beaded with raindrops and had spotted him walking beneath the shop signs that stuck out into the air above his head, his footsteps as rushed and unsteady as the tide of people surging around him. He never knew *I*'s name, just as *I* hadn't known the name of the business before he had rung the office doorbell, for it had all started with a dark green easy chair on a dilapidated sign. The backrest was tilted back seventy-five degrees, and that image made *I* feel like a great weight had been lifted from his eyelids, and he suddenly wanted to fall into a deep sleep. But the office was empty except for a desk and a man who looked like a wet log, who said to *I*: "You can't sleep. That's because your spirit has been in a prolonged state of excitement." *I* begged to differ: "But I don't feel at all excited." He regarded the room with vacant eyes: "Why isn't there a comfortable chair here?" Forrest Woods smiled politely: "I am the chair, and I can be any kind of chair that you wish." At that, *I* seemed to slump dejectedly: "I just want to sit under a tree." Using his professional tone of voice, Woods reassured *I*: "Some chairs are as solid as tree trunks." *I*'s gaze followed Woods's long and slender fingers as they gestured fluidly toward a bright and glossy price list.

I's body, as flimsy as a plastic bag, threaded through the tightly packed jumble of vehicles, darting in and out beneath the bristling canopy of signs, swift and sure-footed, never bumping his head, all of which convinced Forrest Woods that *I* would ultimately be unable to detach himself from the chair, just like *F*, *H*, *K*, and *Z*. Thus, when Woods opened the door and saw *I* standing on the threshold and smelled *I*'s dull and heavy breath, it didn't strike him as unfamiliar, since for a long stretch of time, before he came to the profound realization that he was a chair, he had awakened each morning with an abnormally bitter taste in his mouth.

The bitterness that spread from the back of his tongue all the way to his taste buds and teeth was like a hint of things to come, heavy with meaning. When Woods fell into a reverie, his mother would watch him from a dim corner of their room, sizing him up. His back often bore the weight of that gaze, and since childhood he'd felt it prodding him without emotion. At lunchtime, he couldn't help but ask her: "Have you changed the way you cook this? Or have you switched brands of seasoning? Lately, no matter what I eat, all I taste is fruit pits, mud, and smoke." Mrs. Woods's eyes remained fixed on the television screen, where there was a cooking show, "Steak at 2:30." Her voice was soft and low: "You're mistaken. It's not the food you're tasting, but the oral secretions produced by the boredom of being unemployed." Woods fell into silence, and, one morsel at a time, he cleaned his plate.

That summer, Forrest Woods found himself in an endless vacation, and from then on, the word "vacation" took on a whole new layer of meaning. In the past, he'd thought of vacations as cool, refreshing tubes—people passed through them and came out the other end, arriving at a place they'd never set foot before. But that last summer holiday was quite different, and Forrest Woods, who was right in the middle of it, knew that at the other end of the tube there lay a secret, pitch black room. That room was even larger than the world he currently knew, and he was destined to stay there in perpetuity. He didn't even have to set his alarm clock that summer, but woke up every day at a fixed time, sat himself down at the dining table in the center of the room, and flipped through the newspaper, which was a patchwork of help-wanted ads, until his fingertips were completely blackened with newsprint. He had to do this, or else his mother's gaze would start crawling up his back again.

It wasn't until the noon hour drama broadcast ended and Mrs. Woods had dropped off to sleep that Forrest Woods could finally stick his head and hands out the window, indulging himself in the fierceness of the sunlight. On the two hundred and thirtieth day after the beginning of the summer holiday, the air pollution index, the UV index, and the unemployment rate had all reached their highest points of the year to date, and Forrest Woods didn't think this was an accident or a coincidence. He said to his older brother, Rich: "Ultraviolet radiation and air pollution only affect the people who hang around on the street because they're out of work." But the changing weather hadn't made much of an impression on Rich Woods. With every nook and cranny in town stuffed with the unemployed, Rich Woods's income grew increasingly stable. When he wasn't asleep, he was standing in an air-conditioned room in front of a group of vacant-eyed people, wearing a dark blue or dark gray suit, and lecturing them on the principle that if they could find hope, they would be able to secure employment. As Rich Woods explained it, even if local factories and investments were like water that had flowed past never to return, and even if there were fewer and fewer empty lots where tall buildings could be built, there was no need for worry. All people had to do was nurture a hope as exciting as a fantasy, and they would discover that the things they'd lost or that had never materialized were in fact right beside them, and had been all along.

Undoubtedly, this room was a very chilly place for Forrest Woods, and sitting among these listless individuals, he was amazed to discover that they were all remarkably similar in their features and demeanor. He saw Rich standing on the faraway podium, just as he had glimpsed him from a distance many months before, at sundown, standing at the side of a traffic-clogged road, shouting hoarsely, repeating the same features and prices over and over for "Mobile Phones—Monthly Plans." His voice was always drowned out by a pervasive din, and it seemed utterly weak. But in that room, with its constant stream of cold air, Rich's voice displayed the ability to bring together all of these feeble wills:

"When salesmen can't find business it's not because of their skills of persuasion; when politicians can't get support from voters it's not because of political wisdom; when health care workers prescribe the wrong medication it's not because they don't know enough about pharmaceuticals." Rich paused briefly, and in that moment Forrest Woods sensed that his brother was a hypnotist accustomed to working in the dark.

"Here's the thing, everybody is pretending to be someone else, and nobody knows what they really are." As if he were training a herd of fine horses, Rich called out a command: "Don't think about anyone else, just tell me—what are you?" Forrest had the impression that the room was occupied by a heap of hibernating snakes, but then someone stood up and said: I am a magician. The dry, cold air made Forrest start coughing. Immediately thereafter, one after another, came the tired shouts. I am an actuary. I am a masseuse. I'm an opportunist. I'm a con artist. I am a father. I'm a coolie. I am a female. I'm a child. I'm a cut-rate laborer. I'm a prostitute. Forrest began to feel groggy. In truth, he hadn't the faintest idea what Rich was trying to tell him. Rich simply wanted them to remember that there are times when everything is an illusion.

As the unemployment rate started rising more slowly, Forrest

Woods was reminded once again of the two different Riches.

When the bitter secretions coating the inside of his mouth became a part of his body, Forrest Woods thought he might be able to forget that bitterness existed. But one morning he awakened from a dream and discovered that the rank and fishy taste, which had been growing steadily stronger, now covered his tongue like a callous. He violently threw up in the washbasin, but the nausea continued to batter him like massive waves, and it wasn't until he sat down on the floor and assumed the shape of a chair that everything finally calmed down. "I am an inanimate object." Comforting himself thus and holding his breath, he savored the happiness of being a chair, even though, at that moment, there wasn't another body sitting on his body.

He called his lover on the phone and told her he'd figured out how to break off their relationship. "Believe me, it won't hurt a bit." He spoke in the same gentle tone he used when he was missing her.

She was the first person who made Forrest Woods realize that he was a chair. There had been a stretch of time when they couldn't go anywhere, be it a café, a restaurant, the theater, or the supermarket, because they didn't have enough money in their pockets to cover so much as the cost of transportation. Although the holiday had been going for a hundred days already, neither of them had been able to find work that they could exchange for money. At noon, when people on the steaming hot thoroughfares couldn't see their own shadows, Forrest Woods could walk an hour to her house. The two of them couldn't bear to go a day without seeing one another, even though they weren't in the habit of cuddling, nor did they often feel the desire to converse. On the other hand, the moment she saw him, she couldn't resist the urge to sit down on him. Woods encouraged this new interest, and whenever he went to see her, he would stop off on the way to browse at a large furniture store nearby, taking the time to gaze at the mass of chairs with their diverse postures; and every night, in the last hour before he went to bed, he practiced imitating chairs. At the time, he told himself that chair practice was something he did to improve his circulation.

Nonetheless, during his countless free afternoons, he would sit straight-backed in a chair, close his eyes, and imagine that he and the chair had merged into one. His arms served as armrests, his feet and lower legs became her footrest, and his flesh reminded her of a soft cushion. More than once, she sighed quietly that there had never been a chair as warm and comfortable as he was. At that point, Forrest Woods didn't have the slightest interest in what he was; after all, he had been raised since birth to be a human being, as a matter of course. When she pointed out what an outstanding chair he was, he felt unaccountably happy.

Forrest Woods believed all along that she functioned as a conductor between him and the chair, and if hadn't been for this interlude, during which she never tired of plopping down on him, he wouldn't have had the opportunity to practice transforming himself into a chair. He never gave any thought as to how this phase might end— not because he felt sentimental about this particular time as a whole, but because when he considered the equanimity with which chairs met changes, he knew that if somebody else sat down on him, he would be required to observe the rules of chairs.

Sometimes she sank into him, and he gently supported her, so that she could remain seated and do as she pleased, eating snacks, watching television, checking email, meditating, napping, or talking to herself. However, when she fell silent, she had the sensation of being in a cool and shady underground world, that she had dropped every weight and bodily distress; and a perfect feeling of satisfaction left her incapable of uttering so much as an off-hand remark. This state of mind was not unfamiliar to her, and she knew it was a sign that the relationship was moving toward its end point.

(Her phone rang, and an insistent voice reaching across a great distance told her to report for work at an import-export company. Okay, she said.)

When the reporter on the television news announced that unemployment figures were continuing to fall in the new season, Forrest Woods felt as though the tide had gone completely out, and he was a sea turtle, tossed up on the shore, with nowhere to hide anymore.

He no longer had to make the walk over to her home, because ever since that particular day, there was nobody there in the afternoons. However, as soon as her day's work was over, whether it was late at night or early in the morning, she would take a taxi to his place and, without any explanation, would take a seat on his body. Woods always greeted her with the demeanor of a loyal chair. As the days went by, she became increasingly talkative, which led him to conclude that people who spent long hours immersed in the routines of production were apt to become unusually chatty.

Leaving nothing out, she counted all the reasons, large and small, that she was sick of Forrest Woods. His smell, his eyes, his hairstyle, how fast he talked, even herself when she was with him—she'd had enough. And yet that same day, as she leaned back against him, she told him that when she was resting on his body it was like floating in the middle of the ocean, and all the weight and pressure lifted from her bit by bit. Nonetheless, awakening on the pillow of Woods's shoulders, she addressed him caustically: I never want to see your face again, but I can't imagine doing without your skills. Why won't you tell me how to get rid of you? She twisted around until she could see his face, and he summoned up the cool and dispassionate response of a chair.

A week later, as she buried her head in the crook of Forrest Woods's neck she told him that if she hadn't been able to sit down on him that day, she wouldn't have the courage to look at her own face in the mirror, and she would even have felt apprehensive about standing in line to buy food. "I need to sit in your lap a while longer, so that I'll have the courage to go to work." What she didn't tell him was that practically every afternoon at half past four, the people at the import-export company engaged in endlessly speculative conversations about her ears, her lips, her waistline, and her calves. Some feasted on her with their miserable eyes, but more of them cast disdainful looks at her. This was one of their few sources of entertainment, apart from the afternoon tea.

Setting down the bus fare, she told Woods to go to a restaurant near her office at noon on a certain day.

From where he sat on the hard seat in the fast food restaurant, Forrest Woods stared at her high heels from an entirely new vantage point, which left him wondering if it was really her. A lot of people were milling around, food in hand, eyeing the couple's table and chairs like hungry tigers. She was forced to get to the point: "I can't think of any sure way to leave you once and for all." Lowering her head, she said in an almost inaudible voice, "My sole hope is for you to die suddenly, or disappear forever. Only that would put an end to my misery."

Woods suspected that the orange plastic chair he was sitting on had heard her say this before.

In his view, this was the purpose of vomiting: He knew that many things inside his body had already sloughed off of their own accord, but he had no sensation of it. He was able to press the telephone receiver to his ear and say, "It won't be painful. You can keep coming over every day to sit down on me, and have me arrange myself into any position, that part won't change. The only difference is that from now on you'll need to make an appointment ahead of time, and you'll be charged an hourly fee for chair services." Not hearing any reaction, Forrest Woods repeated his policy that she needed to schedule in advance. He had learned long ago to respond with silence when she was either wildly happy or extremely sad. What he hadn't expected was that her voice would suddenly turn weak and breathy: "So, how much does an hour cost?" He named a price she could afford, and then he told her that her customer ID was *G*. Later, he would use a letter of the English alphabet to identify each of his different customers; but in the beginning he did this simply because he wanted to forget her name.

On a morning when the sunlight was shining everywhere, Mrs. Woods watched as Forrest headed out the door wearing a light gray suit and toting a black carryall. She didn't dare believe her eyes. She had yearned for this day, but time kept crawling slowly by, and the scene in her imagination had never materialized, so that now she suspected she was looking at a mirage. At the same time, she observed herself seeing her son out the door with her predictably indifferent eyes. Mrs. Woods understood herself to be a mother who wanted but one thing, and her sole desire was for Forrest to be like Rich and put on a sober-colored suit each morning and go out. She had scrutinized herself carefully, and after thorough self-examination she came to a decision—she must prepare a lavish lunch using recipes demonstrated on "Steak at 2:30."

Forrest Woods had seen that light gray suit many times before, for it belonged to his brother, but as time went by Rich grew fat, and the suit no longer fit him. Whether Forrest was lying in bed, reclining in the bathtub, watching television, or having something to eat, the pale gray suit was always hung up nearby, and he didn't think it was a mere coincidence, but was in fact a heavy hint from his mother. He knew that this day would arrive in the end.

Forrest Woods never anticipated that such a large number of strangers would call him up in response to his classified ad. With the heading, "For Sufferers of Exhaustion," the small ad was published for just three days in an obscure corner of the paper: "You need to sit down. Body equipped with all the functions of a chair, available for hire, prices negotiable."

On the first day he got a call: "What qualifications do you have for calling yourself a chair?" Contemplating the freshly painted sign in front of him, Woods replied: "To be a place where people can sit is to be a chair." Another skeptical woman asked him: "But what makes you different from other chairs?" Imitating the professional tone of voice he'd heard elsewhere, he answered: "First, you must tell me what sort of chair you would like. You'll discover that only in a chair with warm skin and soft flesh will you find true relaxation. You will also be able to find the most comfortable position for yourself." Although most customers expressed strong preferences, for the feel of leather or linen, iron or plastic, Forrest Woods nonetheless received so many calls that he couldn't be certain whether these people were looking for a person or for a chair. He organized his client list by assigning each one a letter of the English alphabet, while also making a note of any likes, dislikes, or special needs.

From then on, dressed in a loose-fitting suit, Woods went to the gym every day to work out, strengthening his muscles and practicing bearing weight for extended periods of time. He might also pick up some suitable fabrics and tools on the way to the rented unit in a dowdy old office tower, where he would leaf through encyclopedias of chairs and strive to configure his bones and muscles into various types of chairs.

G always came to Forrest Woods's place of business late at night, her body communicating to him its changing needs. By prior arrangement, Woods wore plastic clothing and, after arranging himself on a chair with a backrest, he let her sit down on his lap. As she directed, he wrapped his arms around her waist, lowered his forehead to the back of her neck, and quietly waited for the hour to pass.

On the day that Woods realized he could no longer recall *G*'s name, he knew the means by which his transformation into a chair would become a reality.

"My back has been hurting for a year, and lately I haven't been able to get comfortable in any kind of chair." Woods first heard *L*'s peevish voice on the telephone, and prompted by professional instinct, he responded, "There's no chair like my body." But L countered, "I've seen too many chairs already."

When Woods saw all of the inert chairs that L had mentioned, arranged in the center of the room in tidy rows, each with a space all to itself, unpressured by overcrowding and with no impending events to wait for, he wasn't sure what he was doing standing among them.

"Find yourself a spot and sit down, be with them." L had Woods come to her apartment first thing in the morning, and the heat outside had such force that Woods felt as though he was melting. L had never explained why she was hiring him but had emphasized repeatedly that she had always depended on a chair that she hadn't yet found. "I need a chair that will stay by my side. Didn't your ad say 'available for hire'?" L's supple voice bore the suggestion of a threat. "All chair-related transactions must take place on site, in my office." Forrest Woods imagined the many dangers that might accompany an off-site job, but after L agreed to pay him double the usual fee, he had no cause for resistance.

And so, on that early morning, Forrest Woods watched L's childlike ankles retreat into the distance, for she had to go to work. When the front door closed behind her, the space inside the room expanded and the chair shadows lengthened. He sat down by a peach-wood chair and stared at the wood grain, which was full of whorls, although they didn't draw him into the depths of the chair's interior.

In front of him was a chair made of woven hemp rope, a bit further on there was a nylon chair, behind him was a leather-covered swivel chair, and at the farthest point away from him stood a chair that had been assembled from of all sorts of cans. There was also a canvas chair, an inflatable sofa, a wooden bench, a chaise longue, a wicker chair, a big block of wood by the front door that served as a chair, and, to his left, a plastic chair. Forrest Woods was the only chair made of skin and flesh and blood.

There was not another soul in sight. Woods stopped trying so hard to maintain a particular posture. He unbuttoned his shirt and sprawled out on the floor like a wilted plant. He found that the floor and chairs were equally spotless and that the crowd of chair legs did not impede his view, so that his gaze passed beneath the chairs, glided over the reflections of the bricks, and took in the sight of a number of birds flying around outside. Time seemed to stand still. He felt that for many years, when he ate, slept, struggled awake, confronted the inevitable problems, or expended effort, it had all been building up to this very moment—so naturally, he lay down. He prayed secretly for somebody to come and sit on him, to ease his guilt, but there was nothing in the room but expressionless chairs. For the first time he had achieved his goal of becoming a chair, without having to go through the process of imitating one.

The colors of the clouds deepened, and the moment passed more quickly than Forrest Woods had expected. He had no choice but to stand up again and join L at the dinner table. In this way alone, he was able at last, on this final day of the month, to obtain a substantial sum of money.

"You have every type of chair here. What other kind of chair do you need?" There was steak and hot water in front of him, but he was looking at L's thin little face and calmly hiding a secret, which was that he could not bear to watch strangers eat.

L looked at him hopefully: "I need a chair that can give me massages."

In Forrest Woods's eyes, L and F, J, H, and K were all alike— they were used to divulging all sorts of private information. L said that a year ago she had set out to become a serious collector of unique and unusual chairs. "It was like a brand new door opened up in my life." This was after the sudden disappearance of her lover. She was able to pursue this activity while simultaneously enjoying the fact that people mistook it for a way of coping with depression. When people gave her sympathetic looks, she felt the exhilaration of her newfound freedom. Others looked at her and saw an abandoned woman, but she took secret pleasure in living intimately with chairs. Before meeting her lover, she had owned many chairs and frequently spent sweet hours ensconced in those chairs. Purely out of deference to some convention or other, she had gotten rid of that first collection, because her lover liked to curl up on a huge love seat and read the newspaper.

"Not long after he ran off, I had frequent bouts of terrible back pain. The pain was a constant message that I would not be able to sit in a chair for a long period of time ever again," L said, pressing on her lower back.

This reminded Woods of his function, so he sat on the floor, extended his legs in front of him, and felt his mechanical nature had already increased without his being conscious of it. "Sit down," he said. She distinctly felt the hardness of his thighbones, and the heat emanating from his skin and the beating of his heart combined to create the excitement of sitting in a brand new chair. She rested her head on his chest and told him the names of each of the chairs, and he told her that her customer ID was L, but she couldn't imagine what the L stood for.

For L, only a solution that involved chairs had the potential to cure her intractable pain. She insisted that he explain things. This showed him that her desire for chairs was by no means limited to visual appreciation or mere seating, and although he told her quite plainly that he found it hard to adjust to the unbridgeable gaps between various identities, L demanded nonetheless that he make clear his reasons for being the chair before the one he was currently.

From the look of them, all of the chairs there were extremely lonely, and they couldn't answer her questions. Although she analyzed them in detail, cutting apart backrests and slicing open seat cushions, she couldn't find an answer. Now, she simply needed to pay a fee, and Forrest Woods had to tell her everything, although he did reserve the right to lie.

"The reason is that I made a mess of my life long ago. Living as a chair keeps the ruined parts from getting any bigger," Woods told her.

L was even more interested in his gaunt and limber body, and after a brazen inspection, she found what he had in common with other chairs.

Pulling on his hands and feet and sparing no effort, she managed to flatten his body and slowly lowered herself on top of it. The feeling was like sitting on a soft cushion, and soon she slipped into a vivid dream. In it she was flying on a slow-moving magic carpet.

Mrs. Woods's eyes betrayed to L no hint of what she was thinking. Even though Mrs. Woods was gazing at her fixedly. There was a television nearby, with the sound turned up loud and a midday cooking show on the air. L had a hunch that if she hadn't been sitting right in front of her, Mrs. Woods would have been staring at the TV screen with the same intent expression. L had expected Mrs. Woods to pepper her with endless questions, such as, Had he said anything to her, or, Had he done anything out of the ordinary, or perhaps something about how his body had gradually stiffened before he had completely hardened into a chair; but, like a piece of stone, Mrs. Woods just stared at her, which made the air feel increasingly stifling. Over and over, L related what she knew of Forrest Woods's final condition. Later, L concluded that her light-headedness had nothing to do with Mrs. Woods's expression; it had just been the brilliant white sunlight outside.

"All I want is to find a soft chair to cure my back pain. Forrest Woods's hands are very capable, his skin and muscle are supple, and, as I'm sure you know, he always wanted to be a chair. I have many chairs at home,

all of them obscure limited editions. I thought that living with them would make him fairly happy. Indeed, after a few weeks, he kept telling me that those chairs were pretty good. He said, I've never been happier than when I'm sitting in their midst."

As the dusk approached, *L* stepped into the room where the chairs were lined up and walked through their interwoven shadows, carefully inspecting each one and the area all around it, but there was no sign of Forrest Woods. It wasn't until she lay down on the floor that she discovered him, sitting near a chair, the stiff lines of his limbs ramrod straight. Solid as a fossil, he was soothing to her. The first day that he'd refused food, she assumed that periods of fasting were one of the steps in his training to become a chair.

"But then one day, he stopped speaking and eating altogether, and though I knew that he could hear me, he wouldn't open his eyes. I thought he only needed to get some decent rest, and he clearly hadn't forgotten his duties as a chair, since he let me rest on him that evening, and he also massaged my sore spots. He just didn't answer my questions anymore."

L didn't tell Mrs. Woods that on the fifth day of Forrest Woods's fast, when she sat down and ran her hands over the armrests that were his arms, the cold and rough sensation reminded her of treated wood. At first, she thought that Forrest Woods had been born smelling like a chair, but as the luster of his skin grayed over time, and his legs and back grew as rigid as iron rods, even though his neck and shoulders remained flexible, his chapped skin now resembled a man-made fiber, and she had to admit that his body had undergone a subtle transformation.

"Naturally, it was voluntary; his face was utterly peaceful and calm."

L placed meat soups and porridge in front of Woods, in an effort to tempt him with the scent of food to open his mouth; but he was unmoved, and she knew at last that the change was irreversible. She sat down on a wrought iron chair and pondered at length, but she couldn't imagine how she was going to deal with him.

"When he didn't speak anymore, that suggested that he was determined to go."

L could still remember the clay-like texture of Forrest Woods's limbs and face, which reminded her of a dead moth on the wall, the body slowly drying in the air, ultimately transformed into powder that scattered in the wind. With little time left, she'd asked him to turn his body into a chaise lounge. As she instructed, he faced the floor as if to crawl, his hands and feet supporting his body, and his elbows and shoulders forming perfect right angles. Spreading a patterned cloth over him, she sat down again, and at that moment, he seemed to become completely integrated into the world of chairs.

For a long time afterwards, L often stood in the empty room, gazing mutely at the spot where Woods used to squat down in chair poses. In her imagination, the first time she had seen him, he was already one hundred percent chair. She might have hoarded him forever in her room of chairs. But things had turned out the way they had and could not be different. She was almost certain of it.

"Naturally he wasn't content to stay in a locked room, for chairs need to be bought and sold to affirm their identities. So I sold him, along with the rest of my collection. He must be on a ship by now, bound for another country."

After the light on the wall had faded, L still kept close watch on the changes in Mrs. Woods's confused eyes. At length, Mrs. Woods asked, "So, is he a fully qualified chair?" L replied firmly: "He's the most outstanding chair I have ever seen." At this, Mrs. Woods nodded in satisfaction.

She took the white ensemble L was wearing to be the mark of some sort of profession. After L left, Mrs. Woods started practicing a dialogue about her son Forrest Woods, who had become a professional engaged in chair work. He couldn't tear himself away from his job, but his dedication had led to the opportunity for him to go abroad.

"He may never come back, but what does it matter? After all, he loves his work." Mrs. Woods wanted to say these words to someone, but the days went by, and there was nobody who took what she had to say seriously.

Contributors

Rachel Careau is the author of one book of poetry, *Itineraries* (St. Lazaire Press, 1991). Her poems and stories have appeared in *Notus*, *o·blēk*, *Big Allis*, *Raddle Moon*, *Lemon Hound*, and, most recently, *Plume*. She is currently completing a translation of Roger Lewinter's *Histoire d'amour dans la solitude*, the first story of which appeared in *Avec* in 1990 as "Story of Love in Solitude."

Martha Cooley is the author of two novels, both published by Little, Brown and Company (*The Archivist*, also published in a dozen foreign markets, and *Thirty-Three Swoons*, also published in Italian), and a translator (from the Italian) of prose and poetry. An associate professor of English at Adelphi University, she also teaches fiction in the Bennington Writing Seminars.

Johannes Göransson is the author of several books, including most recently *Haute Surveillance* and the forthcoming *The Sugar Book* (both from Tarpaulin Sky Press). He has translated several books, including four books by Aase Berg. He teaches at the University of Notre Dame, blogs at Montevidayo.com, and edits for Action Books and *Action, Yes* with Joyelle McSweeney.

Mark Herman and **Ronnie Apter**'s poetry translations have appeared in numerous literary magazines. Their translations of operas, operettas, and choral works performed in the United States, Canada, England, and Scotland, have been called "highly singable" in the *New York Times*, "lively" in the *London Times*, and "remarkably deft" in the *Village Voice*. They are currently writing a book called *Translating for Singing* to be published in England by Bloomsbury in 2015.

Andrea Lingenfelter is a Bay Area-based writer, scholar of Chinese literature, and translator of fiction (including *Farewell My Concubine* and *Candy*) and poetry (including the 2012 Northern California Book Award–winning collection, *The Changing Room: Selected Poems of Zhai Yongming*). A 2014 NEA Translation Grant awardee and 2013–14 Kiriyama Fellow at the Center for the Pacific Rim at the University of San Francisco, she is currently translating Wang Anyi's novel *Scent of Heaven* and Hon Lai Chu's *The Kite Family*.

Sawako Nakayasu writes and translates poetry, and also occasionally creates performances and short films. Her most recent books are *The Ants* (Les Figues, 2014) and a translation of *The Collected Poems of Sagawa Chika* (Canarium Books, 2014). Other books include *Texture Notes*, *Hurry Home Honey*, and *Mouth: Eats Color—Sagawa Chika Translations, Anti-translations, & Originals*. She has received fellowships from the NEA and PEN, and her own work has been translated into Japanese, Norwegian, Swedish, Arabic, Chinese, and Vietnamese.

Susanna Nied is an American writer twice named as a finalist for the PEN Award for Poetry in Translation. She has also been honored with the Harold Morton Landon Translation Award of the Academy of American Poets, the PEN/American-Scandinavian Foundation Translation Prize, and *Poetry* Magazine's John Frederick

Nims Memorial Prize for her translation work. Her translations of the works of Denmark's Inger Christensen are published by New Directions.

Emma Ramadan studied comparative literature at Brown University and is now pursuing a Master's degree in cultural translation at the American University of Paris. Her translation of Anne Parian's *Monospace* is forthcoming from La Presse, and her translation of Anne F. Garréta's *Sphinx* is forthcoming from Deep Vellum. Her writing and translations have appeared in journals such as *Asymptote*, *Recess*, and *Gigantic Sequins*.

Antonio Romani, a former teacher and bookseller, has published interviews with authors in *A Public Space*. Romani's co-translations with Martha Cooley of poems by Giampiero Neri and Loris Jacopo Bononi have appeared in *AGNI*, *A Public Space*, *The Common*, and other literary magazines. Their co-translation of Antonio Tabucchi's *Time Ages in a Hurry* will be out by Archipelago Books this fall.

Anna Rosenwong is a translator, poet, editor, and educator. She holds an MFA from the University of Iowa and a PhD from UC Irvine. Her book-length publications include Roció Cerón's *Diorama*, José Eugenio Sánchez's *Suite Prelude A/HiNi*, and an original collection of poetry, *By Way of Explanation*. She is the translation editor of *Drunken Boat*. Her literary and scholarly work has been featured in *World Literature Today*, *The Kenyon Review*, *Translation Studies*, the *St. Petersburg Review*, *Pool*, and elsewhere.

Yael Segalovitz was born and raised in Israel and now lives in the Bay Area where she is pursuing her PhD in comparative literature at UC Berkeley. Her research spans Israeli, Brazilian, and English literature. She translates between the three languages and is currently working on a Hebrew translation of Clarice Lispector's *A Via Crucis do Corpo*, forthcoming from the Israeli publisher Ha-Kibbutz ha-Me'uchad/Sifriat Po'alim.

Victoria Pehl Smith is a longtime faculty member of Brown University and gets a big kick out of fiddling around with language—through teaching, writing (most recently about yoga), and translating. Originally from California, she currently lives in Providence, Rhode Island with her husband, son, and dogs Plum and Fig.

John Taylor has recently translated books by Jacques Dupin, Philippe Jaccottet, Pierre-Albert Jourdan, José-Flore Tappy, and Louis Calaferte. His latest personal collection is *If Night Is Falling*, published by The Bitter Oleander Press in 2012. He is also the author of the three-volume essay collection, *Paths to Contemporary French Literature* and *Into the Heart of European Poetry*. Born in Des Moines, Iowa, Taylor has lived in France since 1977.

Natasha Wimmer has translated six books by Roberto Bolaño, including *2666* (winner of the 2008 National Book Critics Circle Award for Fiction) and *The Savage Detectives*. She lives in New York City.

Credits

Adaf, Shimon. Poems 1, 4, 5, 11, and 15 from *Aviva-No*. Kinneret, Zmora-Bitan, Dvir: Publishing House Ltd., 2009. Copyright © 2009 by Shimon Adaf. Published by arrangement with the Institute of the Translation of Hebrew Literature. Translation copyright © 2014 by Yael Segalovitz. All rights reserved.

Ahrens, Henning. "Briefe an den Wirt" from *Stoppelbrand*. Stuttgart: Deutsche Verlags-Anstalt, 2000.

Chappuis, Pierre. "Ces brasées d'étincelles, ces braises" from *Le noir de l'été*. Geneva: Éditions La Dogana, 2002. "Démarcation de l'incertain" and "Sur le qui-vive" from *À portée de la voix*. Paris: Éditions José Corti, 2002.

Courtoisie, Rafael. "El café," "Las naranjas," and "La cuchara" from *Música para sordos*. Bogotá, Columbia: Universidad Externado de Colombia, 2009.

Hon, Lai Chu. "Lin Mu yizi" from Fengzheng jiazu. Taipei: Unitas Lianhe wenxue chubanshe, 2008.

Laurencich, Alejandra. "Los dinosaurios no han muerto" excerpted from *Lo que dicen cuando callan*. Buenos Aires: Editorial Alfaguara. Copyright © 2013 by Alejandra Laurencich, c/o Guillermo Schavelzon & Assoc. Agencia Literaria, www.schavelzon.com.

Lewinter, Roger. "Passion" from *Histoire d'amour dans la solitude*. Paris: © Éditions Gérard Lebovici, 1989, pp. 17–41. All rights reserved.

Parian, Anne. Excerpts from *Monospace*. Paris: P.O.L, 2007.

Sagawa, Chika. "Kaze," "Yuki no mon," "Butojo," and "Osoi atsumari" from *Sagawa Chika Zenshishu*. Tokyo: Shinkaisha, 2010.

Tabucchi, Antonio. "Controtempo" from *Il tempo invecchia in fretta*. Milan: Feltrinelli, 2009. "Against Time" from *Time Ages in a Hurry*, forthcoming from Archipelago Books. Copyright © 2014 by Antonio Tabucchi. All rights reserved.

Thomsen, Søren Ulrik. Five poems from *Rystet spejl*. Copenhagen: Gyldendal, 2011.

Excerpt from *Father and Son: A Lifetime* by Marcos Giralt Torrente. Translated by Natasha Wimmer. Published by Sarah Crichton Books, an imprint of Farrar, Staus and Giroux, LLC. Copyright © 2014 by Marcos Giralt Torrente. Translation copyright © 2014 by Natasha Wimmer. All rights reserved.

Index by Language

Chinese   140
Danish   52, 54, 56, 58, 60
English   12, 62
French   2, 74, 78, 80, 132, 134,
    136, 138
German   106, 108, 110, 112,
    114, 116, 118

Hebrew   28, 30, 32, 34, 36
Italian   92
Japanese   20, 22, 24, 26
Spanish   38, 82, 86, 88, 120